JEREMY BENDER
VS. THE
CUPCAKE
CADETS

Eric Luper

Balzer + Bray
An Imprint of HarperCollins*Publishers*

Balzer + Bray is an imprint of HarperCollins Publishers.

Jeremy Bender vs. the Cupcake Cadets
For information address HarperCollins Children's Books, a division of HarperCollins
Publishers, 10 East 53rd Street, New York, NY 10022.
www.harpercollinschildrens.com

Library of Congress Cataloging-in-Publication Data
Luper, Eric.
  Jeremy Bender vs. the Cupcake Cadets / Eric Luper. — 1st ed.
    p.   cm.
  Summary: When sixth grader Jeremy Bender damages his father's prized boat and needs
to come up with a lot of money to get it repaired, he and his best friend dress up as girls
and infiltrate the Cupcake Cadet troop in an attempt to win the Windjammer Whirl model
sailboat contest and the prize money that comes with it.
  ISBN 978-0-06-201512-9
  [1. Boats—Fiction. 2. Moneymaking projects—Fiction. 3. Contests—Fiction.
4. Scouting (Youth activity)—Fiction. 5. Sex role—Fiction. 6. Humorous stories.] I. Title.
II. Title: Jeremy Bender versus the Cupcake Cadets.
PZ7.L979135Je 2011   2010040808
[Fic]—dc22   CIP
                                                                                              AC

Typography by Carla Weise
11 12 13 14 15   CG/RRDB   10 9 8 7 6 5 4 3 2 1
❖
First Edition

*To Ethan, who reminds me every day
what it's like to be a boy,
and to Lily, who teaches me every day
what it takes to be a girl*

Wedge of Allegiance

Jeremy Bender once heard that every time a person learned something, a new wrinkle worked its way into his or her brain. Jeremy knew better than to believe this, but for some reason the idea had stayed with him. Sometimes Jeremy swore he could feel it, that he could pinpoint the instant a new one formed. In fact, Jeremy was getting one now, right now, while Paul Vogler was straddling his chest and force-feeding him a fistful of grass in front of the rest of the soccer team.

Left frontal lobe, Jeremy thought.

"I warned you not to cut across our soccer field," Paul said, jamming the grass against Jeremy's pursed lips. "Time to pay the penalty."

Jeremy didn't struggle. Paul was twice his size, and a fight was exactly what the ape was hoping for. After all, there was nothing better to kick off the school year than a good forced grass eating. From the howling of the rest of the kids, Jeremy knew they agreed.

He took a lesson from the possums he had seen on a TV nature show and lay still, almost dead, the only clenched part of his body being his jaw. Jeremy figured that if he didn't struggle Paul would sniff around until he lost interest.

"Open wide and take your medicine," Paul said.

Slater, Jeremy's best friend and partner in *not* playing soccer, hoisted Jeremy's backpack onto his free shoulder. "That's enough, Paul," he said.

"I'll decide what's enough," Paul said, "unless you want to be the second customer at Paul's Vegetarian Eatatorium."

Jeremy wanted to correct Paul, to tell him that *restaurant, bistro,* even *eatery* would be a better choice than *eatatorium.* As far as he knew, *eatatorium* wasn't even a word. However, talking meant opening his mouth, which would put him at risk of being the *first* customer at Paul's Vegetarian Eatatorium.

Slater stepped within arm's reach, which, under the circumstances, wasn't the safest thing to do. "Come on. Let him go, dude."

Jeremy wished Slater would mind his own business. Taking a stand would only make things worse, like poking an already grouchy tiger with a sharp stick. Not to mention that Paul was probably big enough to straddle the two of them at once and force them to eat the entire soccer field, the dirt under the bleachers, and the probably peed-on grass at the dog park.

Paul dug his knees harder into Jeremy's shoulders. He yanked a fresh fistful of turf from the ground. Clumps of dirt dropped onto Jeremy's cheek. Jeremy resisted the urge to thrash from what he could swear was half an earthworm bouncing off his lower lip.

Paul squeezed Jeremy's face with his free hand. Jeremy felt his teeth beginning to part. Clenching tighter, Jeremy ran through his options:

OPTION ONE: Tell the truth.

Tell Paul that he and Slater did not violate Paul's do-not-walk-across-the-soccer-field rule, that they were cutting behind the bleachers to get to the library like they did every day. *Result: "Are you calling me a liar, Bender?" followed by frenzied grass feedings and several days of jeering in the sixth-grade wing of the Thomas Scolari Academy for Boys.*

OPTION TWO: Lie.

Tell Paul that he and Slater *had* been on the soccer field, that they were sorry for committing such a vile act, and that it would never happen again. *Result: "You'd better make sure it doesn't. And just so you'll remember . . ." followed by frenzied grass feedings and several days of jeering in the sixth-grade wing of the Thomas Scolari Academy for Boys.*

OPTION THREE: Eat the grass.

Just open up and take a mouthful of grass, roots, lawn fertilizer, dirt, pebbles, ants, earthworms, beetles, slugs, more ants, and whatever else crawls around in there. *Result: "Ew! He ate it! He actually ate it!" followed by a lifetime reputation as "the kid who ate the grass."*

OPTION FOUR: Play possum.

Lie here, protect vital organs, and keep lips sealed until the soccer team—and hopefully Paul—loses interest. *Result: "You're such a wuss, Bender," followed by Paul lifting his weight off him and returning to soccer practice.*

The funny thing was that option four never happened. Neither did options one, two, or three. That was because before anyone had a chance to stop him, Slater did the unthinkable. He grabbed the elastic waistband of Paul's tighty-whities and yanked upward until he heard a ripping sound.

A megawedgie.

Paul's caboose lifted into the air, his legs splayed to the sides, and he yelped. It was a barely audible yelp, but it was a yelp nonetheless. He dropped back onto Jeremy's chest and his jaw clenched and relaxed a few times. Then Paul stood up, his hulking body blotting out the sun.

Nobody laughed.

Nobody jeered.

A crow cawed in the distance. Jeremy wondered if it might be a vulture smelling death in the air.

Even with his head start, Slater was no match for Paul. After all, Paul was wearing cleats and Slater was loaded down with his skateboard, helmet, and two stuffed backpacks—one on each shoulder.

However, Slater Stevenson's megawedgie of Paul Vogler on the third day of their sixth-grade year might have been the best-timed wedgie in the long and revered history of wedgies. It was perfectly timed because just as Paul grabbed Slater's shirt and pulled back his wrecking ball of a fist, a shrill whistle tweeted, which froze Paul like the "red light" part of Red Light, Green Light.

"Vogler!" Coach Jenkins barked as he came out of the field house. "Hands off. You want to be benched for the season?"

"But, Coach," Paul said. "Slater—"

"I don't care what Mr. Stevenson did. I care what the members of my team do. This school has a zero-tolerance policy and I need my power forward. Now, all of you get on the field and give me half a dozen wind sprints."

The team groaned and headed down the sideline toward the first corner.

"Watch yourself, Stevenson," Paul grumbled. "You too, Bender. The two of you had better grow eyes on the backs of your bony skulls."

"Vogler . . . !" Coach Jenkins warned.

Paul pushed past Slater and lumbered after his teammates, his normally pantherlike gait turned penguinish. As he made his way along the sideline, Paul shook one leg and picked at his tail end in an attempt to de-wedge things.

Coach Jenkins followed the team back onto the field, tweeting his whistle and hollering for the kids to get a move on.

Jeremy took his backpack from Slater. "You didn't have to do that," he said.

"I know." Slater spun a wheel on his skateboard as they headed past the field house. "I had my own reason."

"Which was . . . ?"

Slater peered around. "None of your business."

"Maybe you wanted to show off for Angelina Anderson."

"Maybe I should have left you with Vogler and your grass sandwich."

Even though Angelina Anderson didn't go to their school, Slater always seemed to spot her. And Jeremy never missed a chance to tease him about his *true love*.

Slater dropped his skateboard on the concrete path that led to the stream and glided alongside Jeremy.

"Only those who dare to fail greatly can ever achieve greatly," he said.

Jeremy pushed a hand through his short, light brown hair. "What's that supposed to mean?"

"I have no idea. My dad says it all the time."

"Well, it looks like you *failed* greatly," Jeremy said. "Paul is going to be dogging you like crazy now. Still, I could have handled myself back there. Paul was Play-Doh in my hands."

"Now I'm starting to wish I was the one made out of Play-Doh," Slater said.

"Why do you say that?"

The two boys hopped from stone to stone across the brook and headed down the trail on the other side. "So I could mold my face into someone Paul Vogler would never recognize."

The Glug Heard 'Round the World

In the days that followed, Paul proved true to his word. Without eyes on the backs of their skulls, it seemed everywhere Jeremy and Slater went, Paul Vogler was there ready with a rabbit punch, a flat tire, or a well-placed trip that sent one of them tumbling to the floor, books flying.

Everyone knew the Thomas Scolari Academy had a zero-tolerance policy for bullying, but Jeremy and Slater knew the truth: Among the boys, there was a more serious zero-tolerance policy for snitching.

"What did Paul do to you today?" Slater asked as they made their way through the woods to Jeremy's house.

"Two book slaps and a dead leg," Jeremy said. "How about you?"

Slater held his skateboard by one wheel and rested it on his shoulder. "He tried to shove me inside my locker but then Mr. Palin came along."

"Lucky," Jeremy said.

"Yeah, not so much. Paul put his arm around me— you know, to make it look like we were best buds. He pinched the back of my neck the whole time with some sort of kung-fu death grip."

"Yikes."

Slater ran a hand over the deck of his board. He had painted it himself, an awesome pile of skulls surrounded by lightning bolts. "And that's not the worst part, dude. Paul's armpits smell like a closet full of dead squirrels."

"How do you know what a closet full of dead squirrels smells like?" Jeremy grabbed the key from under the mat and unlocked the door to the icehouse. Jeremy's mom said the small stone building that was around the size of a double-bay garage was part of an old estate. Jeremy's parents didn't use it for anything except storage, but the boys had arranged some furniture among the boxes of old clothing and Jeremy's father's prized antique Chris-Craft motorboat.

Jeremy dropped his backpack and switched on the overhead lights. "This Paul thing can't go on forever."

"Of course not," Slater said, settling into the one-armed office chair they had swiped from someone's trash pile. "Someday we'll head off to college and Paul will be assigned to his cage at the zoo. We'll never be bothered by him again."

Jeremy pushed two stacks of boxes to the corner. "There must be some way to reason with the kid."

"He said fifty wedgies wouldn't make up for what I'd done," Slater said. "Reasoning with Paul Vogler is like reasoning with a hurricane."

"We just have to think . . ."

"The only way would be to disappear," Slater said. "You have any brilliant ideas on how to do that?"

"Cloaking devices are a few years off." Jeremy heaved another box labeled with his sister's name onto the pile. *How many boxes of clothes could one girl have?*

"Will you stop arranging stuff?" Slater said. "You're like my mom vacuuming under my feet when

I'm trying to watch television. We're in the icehouse; we are supposed to *chillax*."

"I'm making room to work on the boat."

"Leave it covered, dude," Slater said. "If you put as much as a fingerprint on that boat, your dad will have a freak attack."

"I already changed the oil and the filters last week. If I show my dad I can take care of the engine, maybe he'll let us take her out this summer. You know, by ourselves."

"Yeah, right." Slater slid his fingers along the hull of the boat. "The guy polishes this thing with a baby diaper."

"He's bound to change his mind if we show him how responsible we are." Jeremy popped open a stepladder, slid off the tarp, and climbed into the Chris-Craft. He took a seat behind the steering wheel. "Imagine you and me buzzing around the lake . . ." He pushed the throttle forward and spun the steering wheel. "Cruising past the public beach, looping around Dome Island . . ." He leaned back in his seat. "Putt-putt-putting through Log Bay while all our friends in their little outboards stare at us in envy."

"Get real, Jeremy. The only place we'll be *putt-*

putt-putting this summer is at Pirate Cove Minigolf."

"Oh, be quiet and get me a soda."

"Grape?" Slater asked.

"Sure."

As Slater grabbed cans from the minifridge, Jeremy opened the engine compartment. The chrome caught the light coming through the high windows and gleamed brighter than a new quarter. Just looking at it made his breath stop in his chest.

Slater climbed into the boat with the two sodas nestled into the crook of his arm. "What are you thinking of doing?"

"Maybe I'll tighten the belts today."

Slater popped the tab on his orange soda. "You sure you know how to do that? That engine looks pretty complicated."

"I found step-by-step instructions on the internet," Jeremy said. "It's easy."

"If you say so."

"Hey, hop down and get me the socket set."

"No problemo." Slater put down his soda and leaped overboard.

"Whoa!" Jeremy snatched the can off the polished wood and dried the moisture ring with a clean rag. "Do you know how corrosive soda is? You could burn the finish right off the hull."

"Sorry, dude."

"Just be careful. The last thing I need is for my father to pull this tarp off in April to find drip marks burned into the boat. Mission: not accomplished. Chances of taking boat out: zilch."

"Chances of being strung up by your thumbs," Slater added, "one hundred percent."

When Jeremy's heart rate returned to normal speed, he carefully laid out a rag and placed Slater's can on it. He took a sip of his soda and set it down alongside the other.

Slater climbed back into the boat and handed Jeremy the socket set. Jeremy snapped one of the sockets onto the ratchet and tried the bolt. Too small. He replaced the socket with a larger one. Still too small. The next one was too big.

"I need the English socket set," Jeremy said, snapping the ratchet back into the case. "This one is metric."

Slater took a gulp of his soda and belched. "Didn't know there was a difference."

"Grab me the other one, would you?" Jeremy pulled

his head out of the engine compartment and glanced at his father's workbench. "It's hanging on the pegboard in the black case."

"Sure thing, boss." Slater hopped out of the boat again. "Anyhow, all this going overboard is good practice."

"For what?" Jeremy asked.

"If by some miracle your father *does* let you take the boat out for a spin, I'll already have lots of practice abandoning ship."

"Just get me the socket set."

The black case rose into view as Slater held it over the edge of the Chris-Craft. As Jeremy turned to grab the socket set, his arm bumped into something. The sodas! They wobbled on the edge of the engine compartment. Jeremy's hands shot after them. As he fumbled with the cans, the soda splattered . . . across the chrome, onto the hoses, and right into the carburetor.

Glug . . . Glug . . . Glug!

"Toss me some rags!" Jeremy cried out, as though he were a surgeon performing emergency surgery. He hurled the cans into the far corner of the icehouse. "And the degreaser spray! Get me the degreaser spray!"

"What's going on?"

"Just do it!"

Slater lobbed a bunch of clean rags into the boat. Jeremy snatched them and began wiping up the sticky mess.

"Which one is the degreaser?"

"It's the green can on the first shelf. Hurry!"

Slater tossed the first green can he could find into the boat. Jeremy popped off the cap, pointed the can at the engine, and pressed the button. A fine mist floated out of the nozzle and Jeremy finally felt as though he were beginning to get control of the disaster. That is, until he took a sniff. Degreaser smelled more pungent than this. Degreaser smelled like ammonia or solvent. This mist smelled like . . .

"PAINT!"

Jeremy read the can. He was spraying green paint on his father's prized engine! He chucked the paint after the soda cans, grabbed some more rags, and began to wipe frantically. But that only smeared everything around into a mix of purple, orange, and green. Even after Jeremy soaked every rag in the icehouse, used a few old sweatshirts from the clothing boxes, and raided the linen closet for any towels his parents wouldn't miss, the engine was still a disaster. It looked like a swirly finger painting by a hyperactive octopus.

He was going to have to take this engine apart and soak, clean, and polish it piece by piece.

Otherwise, he'd be dead meat.

In fact, he'd be such dead meat that whatever punishment Paul Vogler had in store for him would seem like nothing.

He looked at the engine again.

Oh, who was he kidding? He already was dead meat.

Slater knew better than to say anything. He rinsed off the dirty rags, wiped down the drippy hull, and did whatever else Jeremy asked him to do.

Even hours after the catastrophe, the *glug-glug-glug*-ing of the soda still echoed in Jeremy's ears, and any thought of putt-putt-putting—whether in his father's boat or at Pirate Cove Minigolf—disappeared.

Whatever You're Into . . .

Jeremy and Slater stood at the entranceway to the children's section of the Snydersville Public Library. They had always been regulars (most of the librarians had been scolding them for years now), but lately the boys had started going more than usual. After all, it was the only place in town they could be reasonably sure *not* to run into Paul Vogler.

Jeremy glanced at the estimate for parts and supplies from Gary's Boat Emporium, whose motto—"You wreck 'em, we check 'em!"—was printed right across the top in bold blue letters.

Four hundred and seventy dollars.

With Jeremy still paying off the window he had broken with his remote-controlled airplane, and Slater having poured every spare dime into his skateboard, it was exactly four hundred and fifty dollars more than the boys had between them. And considering how uptight his father was about the Chris-Craft, there was no way Jeremy could confess. No, he had to try to weasel out of this before disaster really struck in the form of being grounded for life . . . or worse.

Nothing the boys could think of would raise the cash they needed to return the boat to pre-spilled-soda status. They tried returning cans and bottles for the nickel deposit, but were chased away from Mr. Zeoli's blue recycling bin by Irate Ira, the guy who wore the baggy green jacket and pushed a rusty shopping cart around town. Anyhow, to raise enough money Jeremy and Slater would have needed to return nine thousand cans and bottles.

They looked into returning scrap metal, but the junkyard only paid a hundred dollars per ton. Somehow, Jeremy doubted they could fit that much into his red wagon.

They had tried for advances on their allowances,

but Jeremy's father only offered thirty bucks; not bad, considering Slater's mother handed over ten.

"Any other bright ideas?" Slater asked.

Jeremy shrugged. "How about a car wash?"

"Dude, we'd have to wash like"—he did the math in his head—"a hundred cars to even come close!"

Jeremy stared up at the full-color poster taking up two-thirds of the library bulletin board. He felt a wrinkle trying to work its way into his brain. Something was definitely forming in there; he just wasn't sure what.

"Left occipital lobe," Jeremy said to Slater, who was busy breaking the library's no-food policy by crunching on what was left of the apple he had saved from lunch.

"What have you got brewing now?" Slater was used to Jeremy's crazy ideas. For example, at the end of fifth grade, Jeremy had stretched a few feet of invisible tape across their homeroom door. Unfortunately, it was Ms. Valentine who next walked through. It took her ten painful minutes to remove the tape, along with a good 50 percent of her eyebrows. Jeremy got five days' detention and had to strip, destaple, and repaper every bulletin board in Ms. Valentine's classroom, all the while having to watch his teacher inspect herself worriedly in a compact mirror and draw in her missing eyebrows with a grease pencil.

"Hey there, guys." It was Ms. Morrison, the children's librarian. The cool one. She was wearing some kind of fuzzy fleece that made her look like a Muppet, and she was wheeling the cart she kept loaded with the paperbacks she was always giving away to kids. An irritated expression peeked out from under the electric blue hair that draped over her face.

"What's the matter?" Jeremy asked her.

"Oh, nothing."

"Seriously," Slater said. "You look like someone just toilet-papered your house."

"How do you know what someone looks like after their house gets toilet-papered?"

Slater grinned and glanced down.

Ms. Morrison leaned on her cart and sighed. "It's the reference librarians. They're like a flock of harpies."

"What's a harpy?" Jeremy asked.

"It's a mythological creature that screams so loud it drives people crazy. Those reference librarians get in my hair every time I try to do something interesting or fun for the kids." She looked around as though one might be lurking in the shadows. "It's like all they want is for everyone to sit quietly and read the encyclopedia."

"L-a-a-a-a-ame!" Slater said.

"My point exactly," Ms. Morrison said. "So, are you two going to make it to our usual video game night on Friday?"

"I thought the reference librarians—"

"You let me worry about the reference librarians. Just get down here so I can crush you at bowling. I've been working on my wrist action." She imitated the move it takes to send the bowling ball flying down the lane.

Jeremy glanced up at the poster, which had nothing to do with video games. "I'm not sure," he said. "School's started and . . ."

Ms. Morrison nodded and pushed the book cart onward. "A lot of the kids are dropping out. Pressure to keep grades up and all. Stay out of trouble, you two."

"As always," Jeremy said.

"And, Slater, stay off your skateboard in the hallways. I heard your wheels rolling on the tile before."

"I wasn't—"

Ms. Morrison shot him a look that told him not to try denying it. After she rounded the corner into the children's section, Slater spun on Jeremy. "What do you mean we're not going to video game night? I just got to level seven on Dance Floor Disco Breaker. I mastered the Houdini Hop . . ." He started doing some sort of move where his knees pumped to his chest and his arms twirled around like he was pedaling a bike with his hands.

Jeremy motioned to the bulletin board. "Check it out."

Slater stopped jumping and gazed up. The poster was promoting a model sailboat tournament called the Windjammer Whirl. At the top, in bold, colorful letters, it said things like *EPIC RACE!* and *COME ONE, COME ALL!* According to the poster, the race was being held by . . .

"The Cupcake Cadets?" Slater said, the disgust heavy in his voice. "Are you kidding me?"

Jeremy knew all about the Cupcake Cadets. His sister had been one. The Cupcake Cadets was an all-girl organization that met after school. As far as Jeremy knew, they sold cupcakes so they could go on camping trips. They went on camping trips to do activities that would earn them badges. When they got enough badges to cover their sashes, they graduated to a higher rank and the whole thing started all over again. The idea of it made no sense to Jeremy, but then again, neither did a lot of stuff girls did.

Jeremy examined the poster. From what all the corny people were wearing, the photograph could have been taken in the 1950s. A girl in full Cupcake Cadet uniform—gold dress, orange tam and sash, and knee-high socks—was kneeling beside a kiddie pool and blowing through a straw at a small model sailboat. The boat was making its way through what looked like an obstacle course of floating sponges, pipe cleaners, and straws. Several other Cadets and a few adults stood around, teacups in hand, cheering her on. Beneath the photo it said: *Learn the Cupcake Cadet tenets of teamwork, cooperation, innovative thinking . . . and a little vanilla frosting!* First place took home a prize of five hundred dollars.

That last part was what had gotten the wrinkle wiggling into Jeremy's brain.

Five hundred dollars.

"Enough to fix my dad's boat with money to spare!"

Slater snapped his head back and forth like a dog shaking off water. "No way," he said. "I am not entering some race held by the Cheesecake Cadets."

"It's *Cupcake Cadets*," Jeremy said. "Come on. I know tons about boats. Winning this thing will be a snap."

"You know tons about *real* boats, not model boats," Slater said. "But considering how you botched up your father's Chris-Craft, I'm not even sure about that. We probably can't enter anyway. Isn't Cupcake Cadets for girls only?"

"They can't keep us out because we're boys. That's discrimination, isn't it?"

The wrinkle in Jeremy's left occipital lobe got deeper. His mind went to the boxes in the icehouse, the piles of pink shirts, low-rise jeans, skirts, and leggings.

"I know that look on your face," Slater said, "and it usually means no good. What are you thinking?"

"If *boys* can't enter the Windjammer Whirl . . ."

What Jeremy was suggesting was so off-the-wall, so against anything a normal sixth-grade boy would ever consider doing, that it took Slater a full five seconds to make the connection. "No way." He stabbed a finger at the poster. "I am not dressing up like *that*."

"It's no big deal," Jeremy said. "We score a few uniforms and give it a shot. What's the worst that can happen?"

"But Cupcake Cadets wear—"

Jeremy cut him off. "Wearing a skirt is the same as wearing shorts, just with more ventilation."

"That's where you're wrong," Slater said. "Wearing a skirt is very different than wearing shorts."

"Keeping boys out of the Cupcake Cadets is unfair in the first place," Jeremy said. "So while we're raking it in, we'll be making a statement."

"If the statement you want to make is 'I like wearing a gold dress and an orange beanie,' then mission accomplished, Jeremy."

"It's called a tam, not a beanie."

Slater's mouth curled up. "You knew that stupid hat is called a tam?"

"My mom always used to yell at Ruthie for leaving hers around the house," Jeremy said. "And remember: Only those who dare to fail greatly can ever achieve greatly."

"Robert Kennedy!" Ms. Morrison called out from behind them. She was pushing an empty shelving cart back toward the front of the library, her Crocs silent on the floor.

"Huh?" Jeremy and Slater said at once.

"That quote about failing greatly and achieving greatly. Robert Kennedy said it."

"Thanks for the history lesson," Slater said.

The boys waited for Ms. Morrison to pass through

the archway painted like castle bricks. She made a left and headed toward the returns bin. Slater crossed his arms and walked to one of the library's many display cases. It had photos of kids doing all sorts of different activities. A colorful poster in the center read: *Whatever You're Into, Get Into the Library!*

"Come on," Jeremy said. "We go out on a limb once. If people figure out we're not really girls, we have one moment of total embarrassment. It'll be no worse than what Paul Vogler puts us through every day."

"It's totally worse," Slater said.

Jeremy went on. "Just the other day you were wishing for some way to change your looks so Paul wouldn't recognize you."

"It's one thing to change my looks," Slater said. "It's another to change my looks to a *girl*!"

"But if we can pull this off . . ."

Slater ran a hand through his long, floppy-in-the-front skater hair. "You talk about this like it'd be a cakewalk."

"No," Jeremy said, smiling. "It'd be a *cup*cake walk." He grabbed Slater's arm and pulled him close. "Plus, it's five hundred bucks."

Slater softened at the mention of the prize money,

but Jeremy could tell he was still not buying it.

"Come on, Slater. Winning this race—" Jeremy slapped the poster and moved closer to his friend. "Winning this race will get us the money we need to fix my father's boat. Winning this race will—" But his words were cut short by the sound of footsteps.

Two girls around their age, one squeezing a bundle of posters under her arm, walked toward them. They were both wearing Cupcake Cadet uniforms with colorful patches all over their orange sashes. The first girl Jeremy had never seen before. She had dark hair, loads of freckles, and eyes that darted around like a starving cat's as it sized up its prey. Jeremy did recognize the other one—Angelina Anderson, Slater's secret crush. She had long blond hair, blue eyes, and shoulders pulled back so far that Jeremy figured her elbows could touch.

Jeremy heard Slater's breath catch in his throat.

When the girls reached the bulletin board, they looked at the Windjammer Whirl poster hanging there. "I guess someone else put one up already," Angelina said.

"Fabulous," the other girl said, her voice sharper than the thumbtacks holding up the poster. "I don't even know why we're doing this. My sailboat design is going to blow the doors off the competition."

"You mean 'blow the sails,' don't you?" Angelina said.

Even though the boys were pretending not to listen in, Slater laughed a little too loudly at Angelina's joke.

The other girl turned her back on the boys and sighed dramatically. "All the way down here . . . for nothing."

"We can get books!" Angelina said. "That's not nothing, Margaret." She tugged on her friend's puffy sleeve and pulled her toward the children's section. "The sign even says so: Whatever you're into, get into the library!"

The girl named Margaret reluctantly followed. "The only word I like on that poster is the first one . . . *What-e-ver!*"

The girls walked into the children's section, Angelina with a spring in her step. Slater stared after them until they were out of sight.

Jeremy waved his hand in Slater's face. "Hello? You still there?" He smiled wickedly. "I take it you're in?"

Slater nodded.

Men in Uniform

"I know she's got them packed away here somewhere," Jeremy said, digging through another cardboard box. The trouble was, the icehouse was loaded with boxes, stacked high against the walls, jammed under the card table, pushed beneath the desk and boat trailer, even piled on a loft Jeremy's father had built across the rafters.

Jeremy dug deeper into one of the cartons. "Why do girls have so many clothes?"

"You sure your sister's uniforms are the same ones they use now?" Slater asked. He had cleared a small area in the middle of the icehouse and was practicing kickflips on his skateboard.

"You saw Angelina and that other girl," Jeremy said, tossing shirt after shirt over his shoulder. "I doubt they've changed that design in a hundred years."

"The Cupcake Cadets have been around that long?"

"Actually, the organization was founded in 1953 by a woman named Beatrice Hawke. She was a Midwestern housewife who served as a nurse in World War II. She also baked a wicked good chocolate muffin."

"What, are you an expert on this stuff?" Slater dropped into a chair and propped his feet up on the wheel of the boat trailer.

"No, I read it in the fifth edition of the official *Cupcake Cadet Handbook*." Jeremy grabbed a paperback and tossed it to Slater.

Slater looked the book over. "Where'd you get this?"

"I swiped it from Ruthie's room," Jeremy said. "I read it cover to cover."

Slater flipped through the handbook. "We are *so* not going to get away with this," he muttered.

Jeremy couldn't believe Slater. The guy who just last week was brave enough to give Paul Vogler a megawedgie didn't have the courage to face a bunch of Cupcake Cadets? Jeremy planted his hands on the box he had been searching. "If I told you I'd give you five hundred bucks to walk through the mall in a skirt, what would you say?"

"You don't have five hundred bucks."

"But if I did . . ."

"I'm not sure," Slater said. "Just putting on girls' clothes might screw you up for life."

Jeremy tossed some more shirts over his shoulder. He neglected to mention that he actually *had* dressed up in girls' clothes before. Or rather, *been* dressed. All older sisters go through the same phase and Ruthie was no different. She still had pictures of Jeremy in her tutu, pink sparkle shirt, and Mom's highest high heels. Of course, he was four at the time. But still.

"Five hundred dollars *is* a lot of money," Slater said, thankfully forcing that horrible flashback from Jeremy's mind. "If you had that kind of cash, I suppose I'd take you up on it."

Jeremy pulled a bundle of clothes from a plastic bin that had been tucked under the bow of the boat. "So, think of this whole thing as a dare with a huge payoff."

"But what if we *lose* the Windjammer Whirl?" Slater said. "Then it's all for nothing."

Jeremy dropped a bundle of sweaters on the floor. "Are you kidding me? Winning will be the easy part." He thumped the covered motorboat with his palm. It made a hollow sound like an African drum. "I know more about boats than all those girls put together."

Slater laughed. He sat back down and flipped through the handbook. "What about folk dancing?" he asked. "Do you know anything about that?"

Jeremy threw another armload of clothing onto the floor. "Folk dancing?"

Slater turned the handbook around so Jeremy could see. "There's a badge for learning a folk dance and doing it for old people at a senior center."

"We're not collecting badges," Jeremy said. "We're just entering the boat race. Now, put this on." Jeremy held up a uniform. The rumpled dress was bright gold, the same color as his mother's holiday tablecloth. Against his body it barely went to midthigh. The hat and sash, which he held in his free hand, were a pumpkiny orange. "This is the largest one in the box. You're taller than me, so you get it." Jeremy offered the uniform to Slater.

Slater scoffed. "I'm not going to be the first one to wear that thing."

Jeremy pulled out another uniform. "Then we'll do it at the same time. You change on one side of the boat and I'll change on the other."

"You go first," Slater said. "After all, this whole thing is your idea."

"I have two words for you."

"What?"

Jeremy counted them off on his fingers. *"Angelina* and *Anderson."*

Slater popped an ollie but muffed the landing. His board skittered across the icehouse and thumped against the door. "Dude, you're going to be eating that tam in a minute." He snatched the uniform from Jeremy and went to the far side of the tarp-covered boat. "Let me know when you're ready," he grumbled.

Jeremy stripped to his underwear and tugged on his dress. It felt a little snug, but something about the brass buttons and military-type emblems made him feel official, like a general.

"I'll tell you," Slater said from the other side of the boat, "whoever runs the Cupcake Cadets has a major-league racket going. They make these girls buy uniforms and then they have to buy all kinds of badges for it. Then the girl grows out of it and she's got to go out and buy another."

"Not to mention all the handbooks and pins and project kits," Jeremy added.

"And then they make them sell cupcakes!"

Jeremy slung the sash over his shoulder. He pulled on the knee-high socks and put his sneakers back on. Then he surveyed himself. He felt his face flush and his ears burn. He knew he looked ridiculous, but if they were going to pull off this scheme—if they were going to have any chance of fixing his father's boat—they were going to have to get used to seeing each other in uniform.

"Are you ready?" Jeremy asked.

"As ready as I'll ever be."

"On the count of three?"

"Sure thing," Slater said.

"One . . ." Jeremy smoothed the fabric of the dress down the fronts of his bare thighs.

"Two . . ." He set the tam on his head and straightened it across his forehead.

"Three!" Jeremy leaped out from behind the boat in full Cupcake Cadet uniform.

Slater was standing there, still in his school clothes. He looked Jeremy up and down and then burst into laughter. "I can't believe you fell for that one! You look like such a dork!"

"You're the dork!" He grabbed Slater's uniform and slapped it against his chest. "Put it on. We've got to figure this out."

"What's to figure out?" Slater said. "I already told you. I am not getting into that stupid-looking outfit!"

A knock sounded at the door.

"Jeremy?" It was Jeremy's father.

Jeremy dove under the boat and pulled the blue tarp around him. It did little to cover what he was wearing. "What do you want, Dad?"

"Someone's on the phone for you. He said it's important."

"Did you bring the cordless?"

"The signal doesn't reach out here."

"Can you take a message? I'm sort of busy right now."

The doorknob turned and the door began to swing open. It bumped into one of Ruthie's unpacked boxes. Mr. Bender began to nudge it, but Jeremy leaped from under the boat, his knee socks a blur. He barreled into the door and slammed it shut.

"We're cleaning out the icehouse," Jeremy called out. "Everything's all over the place. Just take a message."

"Are you sure? It sounds urgent."

"I'm sure," Jeremy said.

When Mr. Bender's footsteps on the gravel faded and they heard the back door slam, they began speaking in rushed whispers.

"Get your uniform on," Jeremy insisted.

"No way. Not with your dad around."

"All right, but at least let's figure out our names and a story about why no one knows us from town."

Slater dropped back into the desk chair and spun himself in a circle. "We could be fraternal twins," he suggested. "You know, the kind that don't look alike. Our parents could be rock stars and we're always on tour with them. Tutors and all that."

"What do you know about rock star tutors?" Jeremy said.

"I saw a show about it on the Music Network. Rock star kids are totally messed up."

Jeremy considered Slater's story. "People would know if a rock star lived in town," he said. "Anyhow, the Cadets would Google us as soon as they got home. No, it's got to be something more normal, more everyday." Jeremy leaned against the desk and began flipping through the *Cupcake Cadet Handbook*.

"Maybe we're homeschooled?" Slater offered.

"Hey, yeah," Jeremy said.

"And our parents want us to join the Cupcake Cadets because . . ."

"Because they think it's a great opportunity for us to hang out with girls our own age," Jeremy said. "They want us to socialize."

"Perfect."

The boys spent the next few minutes filling in the gaps, suggesting names for each other, and practicing their girly voices. Slater had a fist on one hip (just like the girl on the cover of the Cadet handbook) and Jeremy was warning him not to overdo it when another knock sounded on the door.

"Boys?" It was Jeremy's father again.

They had been so wrapped up in their work that they hadn't thought about blocking the door better. It began to swing open. This time, it was Slater who threw himself against it.

"We're in the middle of something!" Jeremy called

out from under the boat.

"You're not cutting up my good plywood and dismantling the lawnmower to build another go-cart, are you?"

"No, Dad," Jeremy said. "Getting grounded for two weeks taught me a valuable lesson."

"Good," Mr. Bender said. "The kid on the phone, it was Paul Vogler. He said he'd be waiting to give each of you something before school tomorrow. He said you'd both know what it was."

Jeremy could imagine both him and Slater swinging by their underwear from two separate gym lockers. He glanced at Slater, his own terror reflected in his best friend's eyes.

"I'll leave you two to whatever you're doing," Mr. Bender said.

The boys waited until Jeremy's father disappeared into the house again.

"Where's that uniform?" Slater said, digging through the clothes scattered on the icehouse floor.

"What's with the new interest?" Jeremy asked.

Slater draped the dress and one sock over his shoulder and kept hunting for the rest. "Paul Vogler might want to kill Slater . . ." He found the sash and the other sock. He slapped the tam on his head. It sat crooked over one eyebrow, but with his long hair it didn't look half bad. "But not even Paul Vogler would lay a hand on *Samantha*."

Tuck, Touch, and Flip

Jeremy's older sister, Ruthie, didn't keep her bedroom door locked, latched, or bolted when she was in there, but Jeremy knew better than to walk in on her. Instead, he stood in the hallway and peered in with amazement. Ruthie could talk on the phone with one friend, text two or three others, and IM all the rest without losing track of who was saying what. Jeremy couldn't understand how she managed to keep it straight—she was like some kind of circus seal juggling twelve balls at once. But she was a scary seal. The penalty for interrupting her was swift punishment in the form of a noogie to the shoulder, which she lovingly called a "monkey scrub."

Jeremy waited until there was a lull in the conversation and then tapped lightly on Ruthie's open door.

"Hang on," she said to Jeremy, head still down and fingers flying over the keys. Finally, Ruthie covered the phone with her free hand. "What do you want?" she whispered.

"I have to ask you something, dearest sis."

"Dearest sis, huh?" She turned her attention back to the phone and let him stand in the doorway for what seemed like a year. When she finally realized Jeremy wasn't going anywhere, she told whoever she was talking to that she'd call back. She tossed the phone on her pillow. "If you're calling me 'dearest sis,' it must be important."

"Majorly important." Jeremy took a step into Ruthie's room, careful not to tread on any of the clothing strewn about.

"I'll give you ten minutes," she said. "Chad Bailey just asked out Julia Rozines, and Lisa Proskin totally wants to go to the movies with Michael Spitzer even though she's already dating Peter Martz. It's a big gossip night. My time is at a premium." Aside from having hopes of being a color namer for Maybelline,

Ruthie described herself as one of the three major hubs of information among sophomores at school. She kept up with gossip more closely than the news channel followed the stock market.

It was clear Ruthie took her job seriously, which was exactly why Jeremy wanted to talk to her. If anyone knew how girls behaved, it was his sister. Not only was she a girl herself, but she made it her life's mission to study them like an anthropologist studies mountain gorillas.

Jeremy cleared a spot on Ruthie's bed and sat. "So, do you take down the old band posters or just layer the new stuff on top?"

"Is this what you wanted to talk to me about, Jeremy? Because if it is, buzz off. Big things are happening tonight."

"I'm just concerned that you're shrinking your room layer by layer. Too many new bands and you'll have to sleep in the hallway."

"I wouldn't have to keep so many posters up if someone hadn't drilled a hundred holes in my walls."

"I was trying to surprise you with wall-mounted shelves for your birthday," Jeremy said. "Can't fault a guy for trying."

Ruthie moved toward her door, her hand reaching for the knob. She raised her fist, one knuckle sticking out ready to deliver the mother of all monkey scrubs.

"Seriously," Jeremy said. "I have a question about a girl."

Ruthie's doorknob hand froze; her monkey-scrub fist dropped. Jeremy knew she would soften at the mention of anything that sounded like gossip. Even sixth-grade gossip had its uses.

"*Oh . . . my . . . gosh!*" she cried out. "Are you serious? Jeremy Bender is interested in something other than video games and science magazines?"

"I've always been interested in stuff other than video games and science magazines."

"Like what?"

"Like . . ." Jeremy thought for a moment, but anything that popped into his head—superheroes, comic books, avoiding Paul Vogler—would be dismissed by his sister as majorly stupid. "Like things I can't think of right now," he said. "Plus, I wouldn't want to waste any more of my ten minutes."

"So, who are you interested in?" Ruthie asked.

"It's not really about any girl in particular. It's about girls in general."

44

"Slater has a crush on someone, doesn't he?"

"It has nothing to do with Slater's crush. I'm just—"

"So Slater *does* have the hots for someone!"

"I'm not saying he does or he doesn't," Jeremy said, "but I'll tell you everything if you tell me what I want to know."

Ruthie smiled triumphantly and went back to her chair. "Normally I wouldn't care," she said, "but I'm glad you're finally coming to realize that information has value. So, what do you want to know?"

Jeremy propped himself on his elbows and sank into Ruthie's comforter. "Girls are so different than boys," he said. "I'm just wondering what . . . um . . . what makes them act the way they do."

Ruthie swiveled to face Jeremy and gathered her feet under her. Jeremy took a mental note of how she did that. A boy would never gather his feet under himself. He'd just let his legs splay out and roam wherever they wanted to go.

"I'm not sure what you mean," Ruthie said.

"Well, you're a girl in the know. You're cool. You're mature . . ."

Ruthie almost visibly swelled with pride.

Jeremy smiled inwardly and went on. "Give me

three rules about being a girl."

"Three rules? Are you writing an essay on it or something?"

"Something like that."

Ruthie unscrewed the top of a nail polish bottle. She perched her heel on the edge of her seat and began applying a deep purple to her toes. "This is three parts Pomegranate, one part Winter Sparkle, and a tiny dot of Partridge Plum. What kind of name is Partridge Plum?"

"A stupid one?" Jeremy guessed.

"Exactly."

Jeremy looked down at her toes, pretending to be interested. "Your color is nice, though."

"My color is terrible," Ruthie said. "White is a tough color to work with. You need just the right amount, otherwise it does nothing or washes everything out. I'm shooting for Electric Grape and all I'm getting is Harold's Purple Crayon."

"That book always creeped me out."

"Bad color for toes, too. I'll see what it looks like when it dries." She blew on her foot. "So, three rules for being a girl, huh?"

"Three things that make girls different from boys."

Ruthie inserted foam spacers between her toes and started fanning her feet with a magazine. "Number one is caring."

"Guys care," Jeremy said.

"Guys care about sports," she said. "They care about video games. They care about all kinds of pointless stuff. But they don't care about one another. A guy falls down in the hallway and what happens?"

"Depends on who it is," Jeremy said.

"No, it doesn't," Ruthie said. "No matter who it is, guys laugh. All guys laugh. If it's a dork who falls down, the cool kids laugh at him because he's a dork. The dorks all laugh at him, too. They laugh to get on the good side of the cool kids. If it's a cool kid who falls down, all the cool kids laugh along with the dorks because everyone sees it as an opportunity to climb the social ladder just a little."

Jeremy knew she was right. "Girls are different?" he asked.

"Girls are totally different. Girls stick together. We help one another. We support one another. It's all about caring . . ." She thought on her words a little, then added, ". . . unless you are a total social outcast and couldn't care less about being popular. Then you might laugh. But inside, all of those girls want to be in the popular crowd, too. They just feel like it's out of their reach so they pretend it doesn't matter to them."

"I'm guessing you're in the popular crowd," Jeremy said.

"Do you really have to ask? I'm just glad I'll be out of high school before you get there. Your dork factor would totally drag me down."

"Thanks," Jeremy said. "So what else?"

Ruthie ran a finger across the surface of her desk as she thought some more. She began to draw lazy circles. Jeremy noted it. A guy would never draw circles with his finger.

"How about sharing?" she said.

"Sharing?"

"Yeah, girls share. I mean, guys will lend each other a movie or something, but would you let Slater wear your bathing suit?"

Just the thought of it made Jeremy shudder.

"Would you let Slater borrow your ChapStick?"

"Borrowing someone's ChapStick is one step away from kissing them on the lips."

Ruthie smiled. "Girls would. Girls share everything. If I had a dress and Tracy or Erin or Dreya wanted to wear it, I would give it to her. The same goes for shoes and skirts and shirts and makeup. Everything."

Jeremy couldn't imagine tossing Slater a pair of his underwear no matter how much he needed a pair. "Okay," he said. "That's two. What's a third? And is it going to rhyme?"

Ruthie looked up from her toes. She was applying tiny flower decals to each toenail. "To rhyme?"

"With caring and sharing."

Ruthie smiled. "Ha, I doubt I can give you a rhyming hat trick, but I do have a third thing that makes girls different from boys: focus."

"Focus?"

"Yup." Ruthie flipped her hair out of her eyes. "Girls are like laser beams. Boys are like flashlights. Girls decide what they want and they find a way to make it happen. They just do it. Boys, on the other hand, have no focus. It's like they do anything in their power to *avoid* what they're supposed to be doing."

"I don't avoid—"

"Sure you do. You put off your homework. You lie around in the icehouse with Slater all day. You have no aspirations in life."

"I'm only in sixth grade."

"Well, here's a newsflash, Clark Kent. It's not going to change." Ruthie flipped her hair again. "When you're in eighth grade, when you're in twelfth grade, when you're in college, you're just going to lie around. You'll watch sports and play video games. You'll do anything to avoid being productive. Believe me. I'm a sophomore. I've pretty much seen everything."

Jeremy knew better than to believe Ruthie had seen everything, but he was smart enough to give credit where credit was due. She *had* seen more than he had, so her opinion counted for something. "Okay," he said. "So your points are sharing, caring, and focus?"

"Sharing, caring, and focus." Ruthie wiggled her computer mouse to power up her monitor. One hand grabbed the phone while the other flipped the hair from her eyes again. "Now I've got to get back to my work, little bro. I'll have to take a rain check on the Slater gossip."

"Really, there's no gossip to tell."

Ruthie was already too absorbed in her instant messages to offer him a glance. "Jeremy, there's always gossip to tell."

As he made his way out the door, Jeremy turned.

"What about teamwork, cooperation, innovative thinking—"

"And a little vanilla frosting?" Ruthie laughed. "Been reading the *Cupcake Cadet Handbook* or something?"

Jeremy rushed down the hallway to his room. He sat at his desk and pulled out a pad and his favorite gel pen, the green one. He wrote:

Jeremy Bender's List of Rules for Being a Girl
1. Tuck feet under yourself when you sit
2. Run fingers over things in circles
3. Flip hair often

Out of the Woods

Fortunately for the boys, the door to the icehouse faced away from the rear windows of Jeremy's house. They could change into their uniforms in privacy and make their way through the woods to Dogwood Court, a dead end that led out onto Main Street. From there, it was only a few blocks to the Elks Club, where the local Cupcake Cadets, Troop 149, met on Monday afternoons. Then, it would be straight back to the icehouse to change into their normal boy clothes.

That was the plan: minimum exposure.

Jeremy had made the phone call and downloaded the registration forms. It was twenty-five dollars each to join the Cupcake Cadets (the rest of the money they got through allowance advances, five bucks borrowed from Ruthie, and every dime the boys could find under floor mats and between seat cushions), but that was a small price to pay for such a huge payoff.

"Take smaller steps," Jeremy told Slater as they headed down the trail.

"Paul gave me three dead legs today," Slater said. "I'm limping."

"No, you're swaggering."

"Dude, I'm not swaggering. *You're* swaggering."

"Well, you're loping or something. Do it like this . . ." Jeremy stiffened his back and stood tall. He pushed back his shoulders and bent one elbow as gracefully as he could.

Slater tried to imitate Jeremy as they walked along the trail. Although it was an improvement, Jeremy wondered if going to their first meeting wasn't a little premature. Maybe they should have practiced a bit longer.

"This is so not going to work," Slater muttered.

"Of course it will." Jeremy tried his best to sound confident. "Think of it like Batman."

"Batman?"

"Sure. By day, we're regular boys. We go to school, hang out, whatever. But by night . . ."

Slater swept his arms around. "This is broad daylight!"

"Okay, then by *afternoon* we're costumed crusaders out to right the wrongs of the world." Then he added, "And profit a little if we get a chance."

"First of all, we are not dressed as superheroes," Slater said. "We're dressed as Cupcake Cadets. We're wearing skirts and knee-high socks and these stupid beanies—"

"Tams."

"Whatever!"

"Don't forget sashes." But Jeremy had his own doubts. Although he had pinned the wig he had swiped from Ruthie's closet tight to his own hair, he was sure he could feel it sliding off. Ruthie had spent a hundred bucks on it when she was in eighth grade so she could look like Cindi Sizzle, some pop singer she was crazy about back then. As soon as the fad passed, the blond wig found a permanent home on the top shelf of Ruthie's closet. Jeremy placed a hand on his tam and slid it (and the wig) forward. Slater, on the other hand, already had long hair. All it took was a ponytail to move the mop that usually draped over his face to the back.

The boys were approaching the end of the trail that led out onto the street. Light peeked through the branches. A car zoomed by and Slater spun on Jeremy.

"I can't do it, dude," he said. "It's one thing to march around the icehouse or walk through the woods dressed like this, but I cannot go out there."

"Slater, you're just as responsible for the damage to the boat as I am."

"I just tossed you the can. You're the one who sprayed it."

"If there were any other way to get enough money to fix the boat, don't you think we'd be doing it? We've got no cash and if my father finds out what happened, we're both dead meat."

"Dude! I'm standing in the middle of the woods wearing a skirt!"

"A frock."

"Whatever it's called. You can't make me walk through town dressed like this, Jeremy. I can't!"

Jeremy looked Slater over. His dress fit perfectly (as opposed to his own, which was a little too short for comfort and pulled tight across his shoulders). The orange sash and tam sat high on the left and sloped down toward the right, just like it showed in the *Cupcake Cadet Handbook*. Brass buttons blazed two lines down his chest and white socks were pulled up to knees just a little too knobby. Jeremy wanted to laugh at the sight of his friend in the uniform—it was in a boy's blood to mock things like this—but he knew it would send Slater running back down the trail to the icehouse.

Jeremy felt the tiniest little wrinkle work its way into his brain. This one was right in the center, probably near his pituitary gland. "Do you know what a mantra is?" he asked.

"Isn't it some kind of spider?"

"That's a mantis. A mantra is a word or a sound you focus on that lets you forget about the world around you."

"How do you know all these stupid things?"

"It's not stupid. Monks have been doing it for thousands of years."

"Like the monks who can punch through stone?"

"Yeah," Jeremy said. "Those guys."

Slater hesitantly nodded for him to continue.

"Monks say a word over and over in their head and it lets them forget about what's going on around them, almost like a trance. That's how they lie on beds of nails and walk across hot coals and stuff." Jeremy knew he was butchering what he had seen on television a few months back, but it was more important to convince Slater to walk out onto Main Street in a Cupcake Cadet uniform than it was to get the facts straight.

Slater crossed his arms over his chest. "So what's this got to do with me?"

"I want you to say a mantra, too."

He narrowed his eyes. "What word do you want me to say?"

"*Halloween.*"

"*Halloween?*"

"Yeah," Jeremy said. "Say 'Halloween' to yourself over and over. Convince yourself that today is Halloween. That you're just wearing a costume."

Slater looked down at himself. "Easier said than done."

"Just say the mantra with me." Jeremy closed his eyes and began to chant: "Halloweeeeeeen, Halloweeeeeeen, Halloweeeeeeen."

"I'm not gonna chant the word 'Halloween' dressed up as a Cupcake Cadet."

"Oh, just shut up and do it."

Slater reluctantly closed his eyes and began chanting. The boys chanted together for a few moments: "Halloweeeeeeen, Halloweeeeeeen, Halloweeeeeeen."

Then Jeremy stopped and listened to Slater. The word had a good hollow tone to it. Jeremy didn't know the first thing about mantras, but "Halloween" seemed to make a good one.

"That's great," Jeremy said. "Now stop saying it out loud. Just say the word in your head. Then take a step."

Slater's eyes remained closed but he stopped saying "Halloween." A moment later, his right foot moved forward.

"Good," Jeremy said. "Now, take another step."

Slater did.

"Okay, open your eyes."

Slater's eyes opened. He took another step.

They continued like that, Slater's steps becoming easier and easier until the forest thinned out and the dirt under their feet was replaced with concrete. Before either of them could think twice, the boys were full out on the sidewalk of downtown Snydersville.

Main Street after school was not nearly as busy as Main Street during the morning commute or during evening rush hour, but there were still plenty of people around. People walking from store to store, from the stores to their cars. Cars filling the metered spots and making their way up and down the busy street.

Jeremy could see that Slater was still chanting in his head, his lips mouthing the word "Halloween" over and over. He led Slater past the post office and the drugstore, across Washington Avenue, toward the Elks Club. As they made their way down the second block, Jeremy realized that no one was looking at them funny. No one was pointing and laughing. Slater seemed to be gaining confidence, too. His shoulders relaxed and he was gliding rather than limping, swaggering, or loping.

Jeremy could see the Elks Club on the next block; the American flag snapped in the wind. Something about it felt safe. He grabbed Slater's elbow and urged him forward. The boys picked up the pace.

Before either of them had a chance to avoid it, a figure rushed out of the pharmacy and bumped into Jeremy. Jeremy stumbled back and his tam went askew. He looked to see the person standing there. He was wearing a Thomas Scolari Academy jacket. It was the worst person either of them could have hoped to bump into: Paul Vogler. His baseball cap was pulled low over his forehead and he had a paper bag tucked under one arm. He glared at Jeremy, then at Slater.

Jeremy's heart hammered against his ribs.

Their ruse was over before it had begun.

Slater jumped like he had been startled from a deep sleep and cried out, "Trick or treat!?"

Paul's face twisted up and he said, "Girls . . . are . . . weird."

Into the Cupcake Den

"Girls, girls, please settle down." A short woman with dark hair was trying to speak over the ruckus created by the excited Cupcake Cadet troop. Her voice was way too high-pitched even for a woman. It seemed doubly odd coming from a woman as boxy as she was. Nonetheless, her friendly smile reminded Jeremy of his great-aunt Dorothy, and Aunt Dorothy was cool.

The group of twenty or so gold-and-orange-uniformed girls ignored the woman and continued to chat in small clusters. Although they only took up a small space at the front of the Elks Club auditorium, the Cupcake Cadet troop made more racket than the grand finale at the Fourth of July fireworks.

Jeremy and Slater peered in from the hallway. Jeremy recognized Margaret from the library and, of course, Angelina Anderson. He recognized a few of the other girls from around town, too.

The woman with the dark hair and high voice waved her arms like she was swimming the breaststroke, urging the girls to form a circle with the chairs and to take their seats.

"Who is that lady?" Slater whispered.

"It must be Ms. Rendell, the troop leader. I spoke to her on the phone. She's really excited to have us join. She told me, 'The more the munchier.'"

Slater groaned. "Are we really going to do this?"

"Only those who dare to fail greatly can ever achieve greatly," Jeremy said, trying to keep the terror he was feeling in his chest from making his voice warble or his knees rattle. He pushed back his shoulders, swept his wig from his eyes, and slipped into the room. Jeremy hoped no one would notice them. He hoped Ms. Rendell and the girls might accept them as members of the troop and let them win the Windjammer Whirl without ever looking at or speaking with them.

Of course, that did not happen.

Ms. Rendell winked at Jeremy and waved the boys in. "Ladies," she announced again. "Please, settle down. We have a lovely surprise today."

It took a few minutes, but everyone found a seat. Jeremy and Slater slid into chairs at the widest part of the lopsided circle, against the wall.

"I trust everyone had a great summer," Ms. Rendell said. "And I'm sure we all have interesting stories to share, but please settle down. This is going to be a busy year for us. We have a lot of projects lined up." The girls quieted down and Ms. Rendell continued. "First, we should sing the Cupcake Cadet Song."

All the girls held up their right hands and sang:

"I'll use teamwork and cooperation,

and innovative thinking.

I'll use caring and sharing,

and a bit of vanilla frosting. . . ."

The song went on, rattling through verses about helping others, community service, and civic pride. Jeremy and Slater flipped through their handbook, but by the time they found their place in the lyrics the song was practically over.

When they finished, Ms. Rendell smiled.

"Wonderful," she said. "Now, let's get to some housekeeping. The cupcake fund-raiser begins this week and our first field trip is coming up. We're doing an overnight at Schroon Lake. Fingers crossed it's not too cold by then!" Ms. Rendell went on to talk about other activities and projects that the Cupcake Cadets were planning, but Jeremy could not focus on anything she was talking about. He kept his head down and let his fake hair envelop his face.

Jeremy began to slouch in his seat but then bolted upright. *Girls don't slouch*, he reminded himself. He tucked one of his feet under his other leg but his skirt rode up his thigh. Could the girls see his underwear the way he was sitting? Jeremy held his knees together and smoothed down the fabric of his uniform. He cursed himself for not practicing this stuff in front of a mirror. *How do girls make it look so easy?*

"So, I promised you all some exciting news," Ms. Rendell said, moving closer to Jeremy's and Slater's side of the auditorium. "The troop has two new members this year." She turned to Jeremy and Slater. "Girls, would you mind introducing yourselves?"

Jeremy began to open his mouth, but Slater jumped in. "Hi there," he said. Jeremy thought Slater sounded perfect, not anything like a boy, but not too over-the-top girly, either. "My name is Samantha and I'm in the sixth grade. Well, *technically* I'm in sixth grade, but I'm homeschooled. So is my sister here." He motioned to Jeremy. "We're both homeschooled."

Jeremy took over. "Hi, I'm Jenna. I'm, uh, Samantha's sister. I'm in sixth grade, too. We're twins. Fraternal twins, the kind that don't look alike." He wanted to make some crack about being glad he didn't look like Slater, but he doubted that was a girlish thing to do. Instead, he focused on keeping his heart from pounding right through his rib cage and scanned the circle of Cupcake Cadets. Some were smiling and nodding. Some were disinterested. One waved. Another was picking at her cuticles. Incredibly, not one of them stood and screamed, "Hey, those girls are boys!" or "You two are frauds!"

"That's super," Ms. Rendell said. "Maybe we could go around the room and introduce ourselves. I think it would make Samantha and Jenna feel a little more welcome. Don't you?"

She said the "Don't you?" as though there might be two answers to that question, but the girls knew there wasn't. So, starting with the girl to Jeremy's right, they went around the circle:

"My name is Caroline St. Denis and I'm in the sixth grade." She tugged at a patch sewn to her breast pocket. "I'm a Cookie Cutter, second degree, and I'm into playing baseball."

The next girl went. "I'm Bailey Vogler. My mom is the troop leader but don't think that means she takes it easy on me."

"Bailey . . ." Ms. Rendell warned.

Vogler? Jeremy and Slater glanced at each other. The troop leader's last name was Rendell. *Where did Vogler come from?*

Bailey sighed. "I'm in seventh grade and I'm a fourth-degree Cookie Cutter. I ski and play the cello, but not at the same time."

A loud guffaw came from the back of the auditorium. Jeremy looked to see Paul Vogler sitting there stuffing his face with licorice.

Jeremy's panic got panickier.

"Pauly," Ms. Rendell warned. "What did we discuss about junk food so close to dinnertime?"

Paul shoved the brown paper bag into his jacket pocket.

Ms. Rendell smiled and nodded for Angelina to go next.

"I'm Angelina Anderson. I'm in sixth grade and I'm a first-degree Pastry Princess. Most of all I like keeping the Earth green, but I also like flute playing, fishing with my dad, forestry, fried foods, foreign films . . . and that's just the *F*s. I also like dancing, hip-hop especially—"

"Wonderful, Angelina." Ms. Rendell interrupted her. "Margaret, you're next."

Margaret smirked and began: "I'm Margaret Parsley. I'm in sixth grade, too, and I'm a second-degree Pastry Princess. I'm big into science, in particular aerodynamics."

Aerodynamics? Jeremy elbowed Slater. "Who loves aerodynamics?"

"Uh . . . her?"

Then the next girl went. Jeremy had never seen hair as red as hers, like someone had swapped her shampoo with a bottle of ketchup. "I'm Ericka Lansing and I'm in seventh grade, okay? I'm a third-degree Cookie Creator and I'm into moviemaking, especially documentaries."

The girls continued around the circle but Jeremy didn't pay any attention. He was too busy being amazed that none of these girls could see through his or Slater's disguise. He focused on sitting tall and keeping his ankles crossed.

After the girls finished, Ms. Rendell handed out permission slips for the field trip and gave them all a five-minute break. The girls stood, stretched, and clustered into small knots of discussion. The noise in the auditorium rose again and Jeremy wondered how, with all this noise, these girls could think, let alone hold any sort of conversation.

Jeremy leaned close to Slater. "Not bad," he said.

"Dude, have you forgotten? Paul Vogler is here. We are so dead."

"We've got them fooled," Jeremy said. "Even Paul. We're in the clear."

Slater looked around, then let a smile creep across his face. "It's all because of you," he said. "You make a really pretty girl."

Jeremy curled his hand into a fist, knuckle extended. He wanted to give Slater a monkey scrub of his own, but he knew he couldn't. Not here, anyway.

After getting a drink at the water fountain, two girls

approached. It was Angelina and Margaret.

"So what's it like being homeschooled?" Angelina asked. Her sash was the most cluttered with badges. Things like Fire Building, and Gardening. One boasted Home Improvement. Another Childcare.

Both boys answered at once:

"It's fine."

"It stinks."

The girls glanced at each other, confused.

"So which is it?" Margaret asked. Among the sea of badges on her sash, she had ones for Accounting and Survival. Jeremy thought she should have one for keeping her face scrunched up like a ball of tinfoil for so long. Margaret went on. "Is getting homeschooled fine or stinky?"

"We sort of disagree about it," Jeremy said. "I like it okay, but Samantha doesn't like it so much."

"I think it would be fun to be homeschooled," Angelina said. "Just think of all the fun independent projects you could do. What don't you like about it?"

Slater folded his arms and let his hip jut out. Jeremy was impressed with how authentically girly it looked. "Not enough fun," he said. "No people to hang out with."

"That's why our parents wanted us to join the Cadets," Jeremy added.

"They wanted us to meet girls," Slater said.

"*Other* girls," Jeremy corrected him. "She means they wanted us to meet other girls our age. Girls who aren't us."

"Cool," Angelina said. When she nodded, her blond hair shimmered like satin. "So, we were just talking about getting together to sell cupcakes. We have to sell out or we won't be able to host the Windjammer Whirl."

"Did you say Windjammer Whirl?" Jeremy asked. He hoped the mention of the race didn't remind Angelina or Margaret of seeing them at the library. After all, it had only been a week since the four of them were standing side by side by side by side in front of the bulletin board near the children's section.

"Yeah," Margaret said. "It's a model boat race. Five-hundred-dollar prize."

"That's a lot of cupcakes," Slater said.

"About a hundred each," Angelina said. "We want to hit all the businesses before any other troops move in on our territory."

"Or worse yet," Margaret said, "before the lame boys at the Thomas Scolari Academy hit up all the stores with their even lamer popcorn sale."

Jeremy wanted to say something back, to really stick it to these girls, but he knew that would immediately blow his and Slater's cover.

"How'd you like to join us?" Angelina asked them.

Jeremy wasn't sure they should risk it. A lot could happen selling cupcakes out in public. They could run into one of the kids in their class. They could bump into their parents. His wig could blow off. Anything.

"I'm not sure—"

"That'd be super," Slater jumped in.

Jeremy felt a hand on his shoulder. It was Ms. Rendell. She wore a stern look on her face. "Would you mind if I spoke to you two for a moment?" she said.

Angelina and Margaret joined another group of girls as Jeremy and Slater followed Ms. Rendell. She led them to a folding table near the windows. Something in her expression told Jeremy she was about to say something unpleasant. He glanced toward the emergency exit and plotted his escape route. He would dart out the door, hook a right around the back of the building, cut through the parking lot behind the stores on Main Street only having to hop two fences on the way. Then, the safety of the forest.

Ms. Rendell cleared her throat and leveled her eyes at Jeremy. "Do you know what I want?"

"Um . . ." Jeremy's mind raced for something to say. His legs tensed. "I, uh—"

Her hand extended, palm up. "Do you have your signed registration forms and your check?"

A weight lifted off him. "Oh, that. . . ." Jeremy dug in his pocket and pulled out the forms they had so carefully filled out and signed. He'd felt uncomfortable forging his mother's signature. After all, if they got caught they would be in big, fat *T* for trouble, but Slater was right: Only those who dare to fail greatly can ever achieve greatly. He handed the paperwork to Ms. Rendell along with the rumpled money order they had gotten at the bank.

She peered at everything and nodded. "Very good. Meetings are Mondays after school but we do plenty of activities other days and on the weekends. As you heard, we have an overnight camping trip coming up and—"

"Ms. Rendell," Slater said in an innocent, singsong voice, "we were wondering about the Windjammer Whirl."

The troop leader smiled. "A lot of the girls are

excited about that. Margaret in particular. It's quite a fun event."

"So, how do we enter?" Slater asked.

"First, the troop has to raise enough money. That five-hundred-dollar grand prize has to come from somewhere, you know. I'm happy you two want to participate, but I'm afraid you'll have a lot of hard work to do before then."

Jeremy felt his stomach churn. Slater tensed next to him.

"What do you mean?" Jeremy asked, his girl voice slipping just a little.

Ms. Rendell tucked Jeremy's money order into her shirt pocket and patted it a few times. "In addition to selling enough cupcakes, you'll each need at least three Caliber Badges to enter, and that's no easy task. We don't hand them out for just anything."

"Not to mention all the cupcakes you'll have to sell." The voice came from behind them. It was Paul.

"Oh, Jenna, Samantha." Ms. Rendell put her arm around Paul, who looked up at her and smiled. "This is my son, Paul. He comes to meetings every once in a while when his father is working."

"Nice to, uh, meet you," Jeremy said. He and Slater

made brief eye contact, gave briefer smiles, and turned their faces away.

"Those cupcakes are murder to sell," Paul said. "They're like lead weights."

"Oh, hush," Ms. Rendell scolded.

Jeremy forced his face to brighten. "Don't you worry yourself about a thing, Ms. Rendell," he said. "We'll be ready for that Windjammer Whirl. Cupcakes sold, badges on sashes, everything."

She looked jubilant. "Looks like I have two go-getters on my hands."

The Three Rules of Sales

"Dearest sis," Jeremy said. "Would you please pass the asparagus?"

Jeremy's mother's, father's, and sister's heads swung up from their plates.

"Dearest sis?" Ruthie said.

"Please?" Mr. Bender asked.

Mrs. Bender dropped her fork. "More asparagus?"

Ruthie passed the bowl and Jeremy took a generous helping of the long, stringy-looking stalks. He tried not to wince but wasn't sure if his face was obeying.

"So what's with your new love of vegetables?" Jeremy's mother said.

He held up his fork and looked at the slimy, dripping greenery hanging off it. "Mom, everything you cook is just grand."

At that, all three of them burst into laughter.

Jeremy's father clicked off the news program he had been watching. "Okay, Jeremy, what's going on?"

A look of innocence mixed with surprise sprang to Jeremy's face. "Nothing, Dad. I guess my taste buds are maturing."

"All right," he said, motioning to Jeremy's fork. "Eat that asparagus without gagging. We'll see how mature your taste buds are."

Jeremy popped the whole thing in his mouth. The salty, buttery, boiled stalk practically wriggled, almost felt alive. He chewed it twice, three times, then tried for a fourth, but decided it would just be easier to choke it down whole. The glob slid down his throat like a slow-moving slug.

"See?" he said. Jeremy thought he could feel the asparagus trying to escape but he managed a weak smile. "Dee-licious."

"I still don't buy it," Ruthie muttered.

Dinner continued, the only sounds being the scraping of forks on plates and the occasional clearing of a throat, followed by light conversation about the day. Finally, just as Ruthie was sliding her chair back to excuse herself, Jeremy cut in. "So, guys, I was wondering if you could help me with something."

"Ha! I knew it!" Ruthie sat back down. "This is going to be good."

"Ignore her," his mom said. "What do you need, baby?"

"I was wondering if you could give me some tips on selling things. You know, for a fund-raiser."

"Sure." His mother squeezed his arm. "What are you selling?"

"Baked goods. Brownies. That sort of stuff." He didn't want to be too specific.

"Ugh," Ruthie said. "Reminds me of being in the Cadets."

Jeremy's breath caught in his throat and for a second he thought the buttery slug he had just swallowed might have a chance to make it up and out.

"What a nightmare *that* was." Mr. Bender rolled his eyes. "I was taking those things to the office by the trayload, pushing them on anyone who wandered past my cubicle. How many did we have to sell that last year?" he asked Ruthie.

"A hundred."

"Wow." Jeremy wondered how he, without his parents' help, would ever sell that many.

Mrs. Bender shuddered. "Those cupcakes were terrible." She began stacking the dishes and piling the silverware on top. "We'll hit up our coworkers, Jeremy. Heaven knows I've bought enough of their kids' junk over the years. Just last week, Joan Martelle sold me two tubs of cookie dough to help her daughter's cheering team go to nationals. As if I'd ever use premade cookie dough."

"Yeah," Mr. Bender said. "Perkins down in Accounting has me buying wrapping paper every year. The closet is stuffed with a few dozen rolls of it."

There was no way Jeremy could let his family help. Those cupcakes had the Cupcake Cadet logo all over the plastic wrappers. "I don't need help selling," he said. "I just want some pointers. You know, a few tips on how to be a good salesperson."

"Oh," Mrs. Bender said. "That's easy. My advice is to smile. People like it when you smile." She squeezed Jeremy's cheek. "And you have such a cute smile."

Mr. Bender clicked on the television again. He was obsessed with hearing the weather about fifty times a day. "And give them more than they expect," he added. "It's all about service. You need to exceed expectations to develop a loyal customer base."

"Plus," Ruthie said, "tell them what you're going to do for them, do it, and then tell them what you did. It helps people understand that you are meeting or even exceeding their expectations."

Mr. Bender clicked off the television again. It was before the five-day forecast came up, which might have been a first. "Where did you hear that, Ruthie?" He pulled a pad and pen from his shirt pocket and jotted it down. "That's good."

"You don't become a color developer for Maybelline by just mixing colors in your bedroom, Dad."

He reread what he had written. "I may use it in my quarterly presentation to the sales team."

Ruthie beamed.

Mrs. Bender started clearing the dishes and Mr. Bender leaped up to help. Jeremy's father avoided doing any housework until Mrs. Bender started doing it. Then he jumped into overdrive and typically became more of a hindrance than a help, unless breaking dishes, spilling milk cartons, or dumping filled vacuum cleaner bags was somehow a help. "Let me get that," he said, reaching for the plates.

"Oh, I've got it," she said.

"Then I'll load." He scurried into the kitchen and opened the dishwasher.

"Do you mind if I head back upstairs?" Ruthie asked. "I'm working on a new color—Mandarin Melon. It's sort of a pinky orange color with sparkles."

All of Ruthie's colors had sparkles.

"Go on," Mrs. Bender said. She glanced at the windowsill. "I'm trying a new pie recipe tonight— caramel apple walnut—but it's still cooling. We'll have dessert in a bit."

Aside from doing publicity work for New York's junior senator, Jeremy's mother was a wicked good pie maker. She baked them for all occasions: bake sales, visiting relatives, political fund-raisers, any and every last holiday (possibly even Arbor Day). She told Jeremy that after a long day of thinking, writing press releases, and dealing with jerky politicians, she liked doing something with her hands, something she didn't have to think too much about. She kept her recipes secret but promised to share them with Jeremy and Ruthie someday. As if Jeremy cared about *making* pies. He only cared about *eating* them, and caramel apple walnut sounded awesome.

"Be sure to get your homework done," Mr. Bender called after Ruthie, but her door had already slammed before her father finished his sentence.

Mrs. Bender headed upstairs, too.

Jeremy returned the ketchup and mustard to the refrigerator. He sidled up next to his father and began scraping plates into the garbage can. "So, Dad, about that bake sale thing . . ."

"Don't you worry about it," he said. "Your mother and I will take a load of them off your hands."

"That's okay," Jeremy said. He stacked the plates next to the sink and gathered up the napkins and placemats. "There are lots of hungry guys at school."

Jeremy's father turned his head, a boyish glint in his eye. "There are lots of hungry guys here, too." He broke a hunk of crust from the cooling pie and popped it in his mouth.

Where There's Fire,
There Are Cupcakes!

"How many cupcakes have we unloaded so far?" Slater asked.

Jeremy opened the case that was sitting in the wagon. He triple-counted their inventory as though he didn't already know the exact answer. "Four," he said.

"Four? We've been up and down Main Street twice and we've only sold four cupcakes?"

"Actually, three," Jeremy said. "You ate the first one."

"Don't remind me," Slater said. "Paul was right.

Those things are like lead weights."

Jeremy arranged the boxes squarely in the center of the wagon and glanced down at himself. One thing was for sure. He was getting more comfortable in the Cupcake Cadet uniform. He barely even noticed it anymore. When he went into Washington Deli and News, he was sure that Mr. Aldrich would recognize him. Nope. Then when he went into Staci's Quality Dry Cleaners, he was positive that Mrs. Weinerman would see through his disguise. Nope. When he nudged open the door of Bright Lights, Big Video and saw Mr. Punjabi pointing a finger at him, Jeremy was certain the jig was up. It turned out he was only motioning for Jeremy to fix his smudged lip gloss. He had been wearing Strawberry Liquid Shimmer and eagerly applied more. He hated to admit it, but the stuff tasted pretty good.

The trouble was that no one was buying any cupcakes.

"I can't believe we've only sold three of these stupid things!" Slater cried out.

"Gotcha beat by thirty-eight." The voice was that of Margaret Parsley. She and Angelina had rolled their wagon up behind the boys. "Early bird catches the worm," she added.

Jeremy wanted to call *her* a worm, but he figured that wasn't too girlish.

Angelina squinted against the morning sun. "Please, Margaret," she said. "We've only sold thirty-eight because my parents bought a dozen and your mom took a load of them to work."

"A sale is a sale," Margaret said.

Angelina turned to the boys, then kicked at the wheel of their wagon. "I know we talked about selling as a group," she said, "but I didn't have your phone number. We try to hit these stores early, before the owners have a chance to cram their faces with donuts or sticky buns. Anyhow, I have dance class at noon."

Jeremy had known this was going to be an issue. He couldn't very well give any of the Cupcake Cadets his phone number. His parents wouldn't know who Jenna and Samantha were.

"Our parents are real pains about using the phone," Jeremy said.

"Ugh," Angelina said. "Life without a phone would be a major pain."

Slater clutched his stomach. "Eating those cupcakes is worse."

"Yeah," Angelina said. "They're pretty bad."

"Hey, have you guys been to the firehouse?" Slater asked the girls.

"That's our next stop," Margaret said.

"We could let them have the firehouse, couldn't we, Maggie?" Angelina said.

Margaret looked at a ledger book she was carrying. "The firehouse was our best sale last year."

"We sold them three," Angelina said. "Anyhow, it all goes to the same place. Let's let Jenna and Samantha have that one. It could be our Rainbow Sprinkle Good Deed of the Day."

Jeremy could tell, Rainbow Sprinkle Good Deed or not, Margaret did not like the idea, but she grudgingly nodded.

"Thanks a bunch!" Slater said. "See you guys . . . I mean gals . . . later."

"We're not *gals*," Margaret said. "We're Cadets."

"Okaaaay," Jeremy said.

"It's not okay," Margaret snapped. "*Gals* is the diminutive form of *girls*, and I don't even think *that* word is good."

"I just thought it was the female version of *guys*," Jeremy said.

"And we *are* girls," Angelina added. "I could

understand if we were adults or something . . ."

"Yeah, well, it all starts now," Margaret said. "If we let it happen at this age, it'll just continue." She grabbed the handle of their wagon and started tugging. Angelina followed.

After they turned the corner, Jeremy and Slater made for the firehouse. Now that they knew the girls were having trouble selling cupcakes, too, they walked with new fervor. The boys pulled their wagon up the driveway where a man and a woman, each wearing suspenders and thick firefighter pants with reflective stripes, were rolling hoses.

"What can we do for you gals?" the man asked.

"*Cadets*," Slater corrected him.

"Huh?" the firefighter said.

Slater cleared his throat. "We're Cadets, not gals," he explained. "*Gals* is the dippity-do-dah form of the word *girls* . . . or something."

The firefighters looked at each other and shrugged. "Okay, what can we do for you *Cadets*?"

Jeremy decided to take his family's advice and follow their sales suggestions. Although he hated to admit it, even Ruthie seemed to know more about selling than he did. He plastered a big smile across his face. "Hi there, I'm Jenna and this is Samantha. We're Cupcake Cadets and we're here to exceed your expectations."

The firefighters gave him puzzled expressions.

"You're here to sell us cupcakes," the male firefighter said flatly.

"We're here to give you much more than that," Jeremy said. "We're here to give you an experience. Sure, that experience *includes* cupcakes, but that's only a small part of what we're offering."

The female firefighter looked amused. She crossed her arms and asked, "So what is it that you're offering?"

"Ummm," Jeremy said. He had no idea what to offer.

Slater jumped in. "I'm glad you asked," he said, "because for today only we are offering free truck-polishing services with the purchase of ten cupcakes."

Jeremy nudged him.

"I mean with the purchase of *twenty* cupcakes."

The female firefighter's eyebrows shot up. "Truck-polishing services?" she asked.

"Twenty cupcakes?" the other said.

"That's right," Jeremy said. "It's a very specialized service, and if you act now, we'll throw in free hose rolling and . . . uh . . ."

"Dalmatian walking!" Slater threw in.

"We don't have a Dalmatian," the female firefighter said. "We have a pet hamster."

"Then a free hamster cage cleaning," Jeremy said.

"Huh," the male firefighter said. "Sounds like a good deal."

"It's a great deal," Jeremy said. "I ask you, has any other Cupcake Cadet come around with such an excellent offer?"

"I don't believe so," the female firefighter said. "The trouble is liability."

"Liability?" Jeremy didn't even know what the word meant.

"You know," she told them. "One of you kids fall off the truck and hit your head on the concrete and all of a sudden we've got a lawsuit on our hands."

"We wouldn't—"

"I know you wouldn't," the man said, "but we're not allowed to let untrained people work on the trucks. If the chief found out, we'd be burnt toast."

"Sorry, girls," the woman said. She went back to her hose rolling.

Jeremy burst out, "But I was about to tell you I was going to sell you cupcakes, then sell them to you, and then tell you I sold you cupcakes!"

Once again, the firefighters gave one another puzzled expressions. The man tugged on his suspenders. "Sorry. My niece is a Cadet," he said. "I buy all my Cupcake Cadet cupcakes from her. Already have two firefighters in the hospital getting their stomachs pumped."

The woman laughed.

Deflated, the boys started making their way back down the driveway. Suddenly, Slater turned around and dashed back to the firefighters.

"You need something else?" the male firefighter asked.

"I was just wondering if the chief is around right this minute."

Both firefighters shook their heads. "He's away for the weekend on a fishing trip. How come?"

Slater darted past them. "Forget liability. I want to slide down the brass pole!"

Kitchen Catastrophe

They had barely started baking and already the kitchen was a disaster. After rereading all the Cupcake Cadet activities, Jeremy and Slater decided their first Caliber Badges would be for pie making. Jeremy had seen his mother make pies about a thousand times. How hard could it be? They planned to spend Sunday afternoon baking while Jeremy's parents were out shopping. They'd let the pie cool overnight in the icehouse and then bring it to Monday's Cadet meeting.

The perfect crime.

"Dude, what's the difference between a cobbler, a crisp, and a crumble?" Slater asked, lifting his head from one of Mrs. Bender's cookbooks.

"I have no idea," Jeremy said. He worked the peeler over one of the Honeycrisp apples they had found in a basket on the back porch and let the skin drop into the sink.

"And what the heck is a betty?"

"Maybe it's named after the lady on the cover of the cookbook." Jeremy pointed to the woman whose puffed-out black hair was bigger than a space helmet. "She looks like a Betty. Hey, can these peels go down the drain?"

"Just stuff them in there," Slater said. "They'll go down."

Jeremy jammed wads of apple peel down the drain and ran the water. He figured hot would work best.

"Do you know where the measuring cups are?" Slater asked him.

"I'll look around." Jeremy put his apple and peeler aside and started digging through cabinets. Slater opened the pantry and began pulling out ingredients: flour, white sugar, and brown sugar. He made his way to the refrigerator and grabbed the butter, only dumping a little flour as he struggled with the heavy door.

"My mom spends most of her time on the crust,"

Jeremy said. "She's always saying how great pie is all about great crust."

"Easy enough. It's like playing with clay." Slater dropped everything on the counter and squinted at the book. He flipped to another page. "It says here to make crust we need flour, shortening, water, some egg yolks, baking powder, and salt."

"Go to it, my man," Jeremy said, moving to his tenth apple. It looked like a lot, but Jeremy knew that things shrunk when you cooked them. He wanted to make sure their pie had enough filling. "The peels aren't going down the drain," he said.

"Just stuff them down there harder," Slater said. "Poke them with a wooden spoon or something." He went back to the refrigerator and grabbed the eggs, then to the pantry. "What's the difference between baking powder and baking soda?"

"Exactly," Jeremy said. "What's the difference?"

Slater grabbed the baking soda. After lining up all the ingredients, he found a mixing bowl. They measured what needed to be measured and reread the directions.

"How do you fold in an ingredient?"

"How do you cut in an ingredient?"

"How chilled does the shortening have to be?"

"What does it mean to cream the lumps of fat into the mixture?"

The boys didn't know the answer to any of these questions, so they guessed. It was only a pie, after all. And it only had to be good enough to earn Caliber Badges. It's not like they were entering a pie-making contest or anything.

They mixed the ingredients, broke the doughball in half, and rolled it into a big circle. Then they placed the first circle over the bottom of the pie plate just like it showed in the cookbook.

Jeremy's mother was right about one thing: The filling turned out to be much easier than the crust. While Jeremy kept his head in the cookbook to make sure they did not skip a single step, Slater mixed the apple slices with a bunch of other stuff and tossed it around.

By the time the pie made it into the oven, Jeremy was itching to get out of the kitchen. Sure, the thing in the pie tin looked more like something his father might have fished out of the rain gutter than an actual pie, but things going into the oven always looked different than when they came out. Even Jeremy knew that. Anyhow, food was all about taste, right? And the pie had forty-five minutes of baking to figure it all out.

Slater glanced from the cookbook to the clock and back again. "So it's got to be in the oven until four o'clock at three hundred and fifty degrees," he said.

Jeremy read the note his mother had left. "Shoot, my parents will be home by then."

Slater flipped through the cookbook. "What if we were to—"

Jeremy felt a wrinkle work its way into his brain. This one came lightning-fast. "Kick up the temperature and cut the time in half?"

"It comes out to the same amount of heat," Slater offered.

"Perfect!" Jeremy cranked the dial to full blast and set the oven timer for twenty minutes. Then the boys raced to Jeremy's room, where they started planning where to sell cupcakes next.

Pie Time

A high-pitched shrieking came through Jeremy's bed-room door.

Slater's head poked up over the edge of his new issue of *Rad-Sk8r Magazine*. "What is that *noise*— some new techno band your sister is into?"

"Ruthie's not home," Jeremy said. "It sounds like Daylight Savings when my father changes the batteries in the . . ."

The boys looked at each other wide-eyed and cried out: "Smoke detector!"

Jeremy and Slater flung open the bedroom door and pounded down the stairs. Smoke was pouring from the oven, and water was overflowing the sink and spilling onto the floor. Slater grabbed two pot holders and pulled the scorched pie from the oven. Jeremy opened a bunch of windows while Slater fanned at the alarm with his magazine. By the time everything was under control, the murky water from the sink had soaked the Spanish tile, the Brazilian Cherry hardwood, and the Persian rug.

The boys had barely gotten the pie to the safety of the icehouse and started cleaning up the disaster when Jeremy's parents walked through the front door, arms loaded with grocery bags.

After the initial scream, Mrs. Bender sent Slater home. Jeremy had to mop up the water and scour every surface of the kitchen while Mr. Bender snaked the drain, clearing it of ten apples' worth of peels. All the while, his parents chatted with him. He didn't know why his parents called it a chat; a chat usually went two ways. This was only going *one* way with lots of questions he was not allowed to answer. Questions like, "What were you thinking?" and "How could you be so careless?"

His father decided a punishment was in order and made him clean out the clogged gutters around the house. While he was up there, his father set him to the task of fixing the loose shutter. And, of course, when he came down, there was the matter of touching up the faded paint on the shed. Jeremy noticed that his punishment took the form of all the jobs his *father* normally did, but he knew better than to point this out.

Later on, after everything was set right and Jeremy was sprawled across his bed in exhaustion, his mom tapped on his door.

"Yeah?"

She sat next to him. "Just checking up on you."

"Doing super," Jeremy said. He knew he shouldn't be mad at his mother—it wasn't her fault he and Slater had destroyed the kitchen and surrounding rooms—but his words came out sounding terse.

His mother rubbed his sore shoulder. "So, what's with your sudden interest in pie making?"

The funny thing was that of all the questions that had been posed to him in the past few hours, this was the one he could not answer. After all, what would he say? *"Um, Slater and I are dressing up as Cupcake Cadets in order to win a contest but we have to earn three Caliber Badges first"*?

"We were bored," he offered.

"You were bored?"

"And hungry," Jeremy added. "We were bored and hungry . . . and in the mood for pie."

Jeremy's mom smiled. "Dangerous combination," she said. "There was this one time in college when I tried to bake cookies in my dorm using aluminum foil and a hot plate. It wasn't pretty." She tousled his hair. "So what happened to your pie?"

"It was burned pretty badly so we tossed it into the woods. I figured the squirrels would enjoy the blackened crust more than we would."

His mother laughed. "No doubt. Maybe it'll keep those little thugs from gnawing through our garbage cans."

Fortunately, the pie was safe. It was as safe as could be, under lock and key in the icehouse. Sure, they had to scrape off all the burned parts. Sure, the thing ended up looking like an exploded bowl of dirt and dried leaves. But how many kids at the Thomas Scolari Academy for Boys could say they had ever baked an actual pie that actual people were going to eat?

When the boys got to the Cupcake Cadet meeting the next day, Ms. Rendell gave their pie a concerned, if not sympathetic, look. She set it down on a table near the windows. Paul scurried about, fanning piles of napkins and arranging paper plates in alternating colors. He stuffed a fistful of red plastic forks into a large cup so they seemed to bloom like a flower.

"I didn't know Paul had such domestic skills," Jeremy whispered to Slater.

"Must be from growing up around so many Cadets," Slater said.

"Or by running Paul's Vegetarian Eatatorium. I heard they got a good write-up in last week's food section."

Ms. Rendell moved in front of the table. "I'm sorry we don't have any beverages," she said. "I had no idea Jenna and Samantha were bringing a treat today. I suppose we'll take turns at the drinking fountain."

Her eyes moved to the table and her nose wrinkled up. "This is a very odd-looking pie. Would you mind telling us a little about it before we have a taste?"

Jeremy and Slater stood in front of the table. The other Cupcake Cadets clustered around. Their noses scrunched up just like Ms. Rendell's.

"It's an old family recipe," Jeremy said. "It might look a little strange, but it's totally scrumptious. A lot of love went into this pie."

"And a lot of history," Slater added. "Our mother's great-great-great-great-however-many-times-grandmother came over on the *Mayflower*. Legend has it that this is the recipe the Pilgrims used during the first Thanksgiving dinner."

Jeremy was impressed. He had no idea where Slater had come up with that one, but it sounded really good.

The girls peered more closely at the brown mass that overflowed the pie plate.

"Why does it smell like garlic bread?" Angelina asked.

"How come the apples are poking up through the crust?" Bailey asked. She turned to her mother. "Is that a branch sticking up there?"

"Manners, girls," Ms. Rendell said. "This is Jenna and Samantha's first Caliber Badge. Let's not cast a shadow over them."

"I think it looks great," Paul said, rubbing his hands together.

"You'd eat a barrel of toenail clippings if someone gave you a spoon," Bailey said.

Paul shot a wicked glare at his sister as the rest of the troop moaned in disgust.

"Looks can be deceiving," Ms. Rendell said. "We're sharing a piece of history here."

"I think we're *smelling* a piece of history, too," Margaret muttered.

"Everyone grab a plate," Ms. Rendell said cheerfully. "I'll give each of you a slice and we'll all take our first bite at the same time. We can experience history together, like any good Cupcake Cadet troop should. After all . . ." Ms. Rendell waited for a response.

"Cupcakes in the pan together bake together," the girls said at once.

Ms. Rendell took a knife and served a wedge of pie to each girl. Everyone stood around, forks over plates, worried expressions on faces. All with the exception of Paul, who practically had drool dripping down his chin. When Ms. Rendell saw how large a slice he had gotten his hands on, she shook her head and swapped his plate with her own. "What did we say about portioning?" she said in a loud whisper.

A few of the girls snickered.

"Mom!" Paul moaned.

Jeremy couldn't help but smile. After all, an entire troop of Cupcake Cadets was about to taste the pie that he and Slater made with their own two (well, actually four) hands. He had never felt like this before, like so many people were about to benefit from his hard work.

At least that's how he felt until the first girl bolted for the bathroom.

It was Cheryl Cahill, a sweet brown-haired fifth grader with big blue eyes. She dropped her plate on the table and set some sort of auditorium-to-bathroom track record. Within seconds the entire troop was rushing for the bathroom. That included Ms. Rendell, who authorized the use of the boys' room like it was some kind of wartime emergency. Paul held the door open for them in between his own bouts in the stall.

"If that pie was served at the first Thanksgiving," one of the girls cried out, "it's a miracle the Native Americans didn't march those Pilgrims right back on the *Mayfl*—" But she could not finish her sentence because she was busy dashing back into the bathroom a second time.

Jeremy fired a look at Slater. "What did you put in that pie?"

Slater shrugged. "I threw in a bunch of extra ingredients. You know, to spruce the thing up."

"That was last year's New York State Fair award-winning pie recipe!" Jeremy hissed. "It didn't need any sprucing up."

"Well, that's obvious now." Slater shoved his hands into his pockets and stared down at his sneakers.

After Ms. Rendell gathered herself together and helped out a few of the more nauseated girls, she ended the meeting early. "I'm so sorry." She dabbed at her mouth with a white handkerchief. "I can't award you Pie-Making badges for that effort."

Ms. Rendell tried to explain, but before she could get out another word she had to dart back to the bathroom herself.

Polly Wanna Cupcake?

"We're never going to sell all these cupcakes," Slater said, kicking a rock ahead of him as they made their way back toward Jeremy's house. "I thought for sure those old ladies at the jewelry store would buy something."

Jeremy tugged on the heavy wagon so it popped the curb onto the sidewalk. "They were total harpies. Who cares about fingerprints on display cases?"

"Fingerprints, schmingerprints," Slater said.

The boys made their way up Mountain Avenue and took a right onto Oakland.

"So, how are we going to sell all these things?" Slater asked.

"We still have a few weeks." Jeremy grabbed a cupcake and studied the wrapper. "I just wonder how they get them to stay fresh for so long. This Peanut Butter Graham Cracker Kazoo doesn't expire for more than a year."

"Must be Cupcake Cadet magic." Jeremy dropped the treat back into the wagon with a thud. "That and loads of preservatives."

"Preservatives *are* magic," Slater said. "How else could bacon stay fresh until after my next birthday?"

As they turned onto Waverly, Jeremy heard the sound of bike tires humming on pavement. He spun around and saw the last person in the world he wanted to see.

Paul Vogler.

Memories of earlier that day, when Paul had kicked his heel as he was walking down the hall, rushed to Jeremy's mind. He had tripped and his books went flying, one of which hit Mr. Palin right in the back of the head.

Paul stood on his pedals and coasted toward them. He began to circle around Jeremy and Slater. Slater picked up the pace and Jeremy matched him. The forest was at the end of the block, and something about it felt safe. The trouble was that with the wagon weighed down with cupcakes and Paul on his BMX, there was zero chance for a quick getaway.

"Hey," Paul said. He looped a figure eight, then popped a wheelie. Jeremy wondered if he was showing off. When Paul hopped his bike in the air and spun his handlebars around, Jeremy knew he was. "Where do you two live? I've never seen you around town."

Jeremy kept pulling the wagon, his head down. Slater, on the other hand, was a bit more confident. "What're you, the mayor or something?"

"No, I just . . ." Paul looped around again and started hopping his bike on its front tire. "Any luck selling those things?"

Visions of all their cupcakes stuffed into a sewer drain or littered across Main Street for cars to run over flashed through Jeremy's mind. "Not much," he said.

"Hey, what's the rush?" Paul said. He bumped his front tire into the wagon and brought it to a halt. "I want to buy a few."

Jeremy glanced at Slater, who shrugged. "How many do you want?" he asked.

Paul shrugged. "Three?"

Jeremy stopped and lifted the flap of the box. "They're a buck-fifty apiece."

"I have the money if that's what you're worried about." He dug into his pocket and pulled out a five. "You got change?"

"Only singles," Slater said.

"Then I guess I'll only get two."

Jeremy felt to make sure his wig wasn't crooked. "How about four?" he suggested.

"I've only got five bucks. Four cupcakes would come to six."

"I'll tell you what," Jeremy said. He figured if Paul hadn't recognized them by now, he might as well swing for the fences. "I'll give you four cupcakes for five dollars if you lay off those two kids at your school. What are their names?" He turned to Slater.

"Oh, yeah," Slater said. "Jeremy Bender and Slater— Slater— Slater—" He began to snap his fingers as if the name had escaped his mind.

"Stevenson?" Paul asked.

"Stevenson!" Slater said. "Yeah, lay off those guys and we'll give you a discount: four for five dollars."

"What do you care about those guys?" Paul asked. "Do you *like* them or something?"

"No!" Jeremy and Slater said at once.

"We just know them, that's all," Jeremy added. "I'll tell you what. Lay off Jeremy and Slater and we'll give you *two* extra cupcakes."

"Five cupcakes for five bucks?" Paul's eyes narrowed and he looked Jeremy up and down. "Crush or not, it's a deal. I'll take two Peanut Butter Graham Cracker Kazoos, a Vanilla Banana Boat, and two Chocolate Marshmallow Fluff Puffs."

Jeremy felt the stale air go out of him. He dug through the box until he found the right items. Even though they were down two and a half dollars, it was the best deal he could have imagined. Jeremy stuffed the money into his pocket. Then he stopped.

"Wait a second," Jeremy said. "I thought you told us these things were terrible."

Paul had already pulled off the wrapper and stuffed the Vanilla Banana Boat in his mouth. "I never said they were terrible," he said, crumbs and pudding splattering from his mouth. "I said they were like lead weights."

"So, why don't you buy from your sister?" Slater asked.

"Yeah, I'm sure Bailey's got a load of them to get rid of," Jeremy added.

Paul was already unwrapping his second cupcake; this one was a Chocolate Marshmallow Fluff Puff. "I like lead weights. My mother, on the other hand . . ." He patted his stomach. "She doesn't like me liking them."

"Speaking of your mother," Jeremy said. "How come—"

"How come we have different last names?" By now, the chocolate and marshmallow were covering Paul's face from his nose to his chin.

"Uh, yeah," Jeremy said, trying not to gag (or get his hands or feet too close to Paul's mouth).

"My dad's name is Vogler. Paul Vogler, Junior, in fact. I'm the third. My mom never changed her name when they got married. She's a lawyer. Says it was a professional thing. You didn't think being a Cupcake Cadet troop leader was her full-time job, did you?" Paul leaned forward over his handlebars and looked at them intently. "So, what was up with that pie the other day? Were you trying to poison everyone?"

"Hey," Slater said. "That's a family recipe!"

"Maybe if your family has no taste buds." Paul burst into laughter and two of his remaining cupcakes tumbled to the ground. "That pie was the worst thing I ever ate. It was worse than dirt."

"Is it worse than eating the grass from the soccer field?" Jeremy asked.

"What?" Paul said, suddenly turning serious.

"We get the point," Slater said, changing the subject. "The pie was terrible. You don't need to rub it in."

"What's to rub in?" Paul said. "I think it was the funniest thing ever. You guys rock." And with that, Paul picked up his cupcakes, deposited them in his backpack, and pedaled off. "Oh," he called over his shoulder. "Laying off your *boyfriends*, Bender and Stevenson? That only lasts through the end of the week. Any time you want to extend it, you know where to go."

Once Paul was a safe distance away, Slater turned to Jeremy. "What was with that grass-from-the-soccer-field stuff?" Slater asked. "You trying to get us busted?"

"Sorry, it just slipped out," Jeremy said. "But see? We've more than doubled our sales figures. We've sold nine cupcakes."

"Super . . . dee . . . duper, " Slater said.

"Come on," Jeremy said. "It could be worse. . . ."

"Yeah, but if we keep selling them at a buck apiece . . ." Slater did some quick calculations in his head. "We'll *owe* a hundred bucks when we're done!"

"Having Paul off our backs for a few months is

worth a hundred bucks," Jeremy said.

"You think Vogler is going to honor our agreement? He'll be on us worse than stink on a dirty skunk."

"Actually . . ." Jeremy said. He wanted to say that skunks are clean animals, but the sight of Slater dressed as a Cupcake Cadet suddenly made him want to laugh. He and his best friend had just outwitted the biggest bully in school—and they had done it dressed as girls.

Stick and Move

"All right, ladies," Ms. Rendell called out in her high-pitched voice. She held an umbrella in one hand and wielded a field hockey stick in the other. She paced up and down the wet grass and pointed the stick at the girls as she spoke. "We are about to go to war."

"What happened to the tenets of a good Cupcake Cadet?" Jeremy asked under his breath. The drizzle was working its way under his wig. The cold water felt funny on his scalp.

"Yeah," Slater added. "What about all the caring, sharing, and vanilla frosting?"

"Forget vanilla frosting," Angelina muttered. "Mrs.

Sanchez from Troop 224 and Ms. Rendell can't stand each other."

"Putting them together . . ." Margaret tightened her ponytail and popped her mouth guard between her teeth. "You ever drop a pack of Mentos into Diet Coke?"

"Ka-blooey," Angelina whispered.

"What's their beef?" Jeremy asked.

"Beef?" Angelina looked at him, the rain already matting down her hair. "I'm a vegetarian."

"No, I mean what's the trouble between them?"

"I know what beef means," Angelina whispered. "They used to be in Cadets together. From what I've heard the two of them never got along."

"Now they live their old rivalry through us," Margaret added.

"More like they take it out on us," Angelina said.

"This is not just a game," Ms. Rendell went on. She glared across the soaked field at a woman who could only have been Mrs. Sanchez. She was wearing a bright red tracksuit. She was tall, slender, and had way too much makeup on for a woman who was supposed to be coaching a sports team. She was pacing in front of her Cadets—the girls of Troop 224, who wore red sashes as opposed to their orange ones. The way her arms were flailing about, Jeremy figured she was giving a similar "pep talk" to her girls.

"This is not some . . ." Ms. Rendell searched for the word. ". . . some stroll in the park. This is—"

A hand in the front shot up.

"Not now, Cheryl," Ms. Rendell said.

The hand shot up again, this time more urgently.

"I said not now."

"But, I've got to go to the bathroom," she whined, hopping up and down. "Like, really bad."

Ms. Rendell gestured impatiently toward the restrooms with her field hockey stick. "Be quick about it." She watched Cheryl dart down the path until she was near the field house. Two more of the smaller girls darted after her. "Now, where was I?"

"Stroll in the park?" Angelina offered.

"Yes!" Ms. Rendell barked. "This is not some stroll in the park. This is serious business. This is about troop pride, personal achievement, and reaching your goals. Now get out there and win! A victory means Sport Star Caliber Badges for everyone!"

Jeremy and Slater glanced at each other, smiles spreading across their faces. How hard could it be to beat a bunch of girls at field hockey?

The field was muddier than it looked. Jeremy's sneakers squished into the turf with each step. He sidled up next to Slater. "Angelina looks cute in her goalie gear, huh?"

"Zip it," Slater said, "or I'll make sure you look cute in your hospital bed."

"So, do you know the rules of this game?"

"Nope."

"So . . . we . . . should . . ."

"Pass the ball to someone else whenever we get it?" Slater suggested.

Jeremy squeezed the thick handle of his field hockey stick. He liked the heft of it in his hands. "How hard can it be?" he said. "Get it in the net and you're good."

Slater nodded. "It's just like soccer."

"Plus," Jeremy added, "there's a badge in it for us."

"You know, dude," Slater said, "I never realized how breezy things get wearing a skirt. Might have to get me a pair of leggings soon."

Jeremy looked at Slater in horror.

"What?" Slater said. "Ms. Rendell saw the goose bumps on my thighs and suggested I get a pair. They come in all kinds of colors."

"Just focus on the game, okay?"

They clicked sticks together like old pros (at least that's how Jeremy imagined old pros would do it) and trotted after the other girls to the center of the field. If Jeremy had learned anything from their pie-making fiasco, it was that the idea that doing something as a team felt much better than doing it alone. That's how he felt now as he lined up alongside the other girls of Troop 149.

That is, until Troop 224 lined up opposite them. It had been hard to get a close look at them from all the way across the field, but when they came closer Jeremy realized just how big these girls were. They were massive, like Mrs. Sanchez recruited NFL stars for her Cupcake Cadet troop.

"Ummm," Jeremy said to Margaret, who happened to be standing next to him. "What's our record against this team?"

"Including last year's game, which never actually ended . . ." Margaret thought about it for a moment. "Zero and six."

"Why didn't last year's game end?" Slater asked.

"Sophie from Troop 224 busted Kathi Bartley's nose. She had to be rushed to the emergency room and we were left one player short."

A monstrous girl lowered her shoulders in front of Jeremy. She had a streak of black grease paint under each eye and her forearms rippled with every squeeze of her hockey stick. She dug her cleats into the mud. "Know why my sash is red?" the girl asked him in a gravelly voice.

Jeremy lowered his own stick. All of a sudden, it felt heavy in his hands. "Uh, why?" he said.

"So your blood won't show." She grinned and Jeremy could swear he saw missing teeth. He wasn't sure even the bravest of dentists would go near this girl's mouth. He looked at her scarlet sash. Stitched in bright yellow, cursive letters was the name *Sophie*.

Before he had a chance to change his position on the field, the whistle blew. In a flash, Sophie's shoulder struck Jeremy's chest. His feet left the ground and he landed heavily in the mud. Before Jeremy could catch his breath, Sophie had passed the ball to another girl and Troop 224 had scored.

"One to zero!" Mrs. Sanchez called out. "Yeah, girls! We got 'em!"

"My girls just need warming up," Ms. Rendell called back.

"More like body bags," Sophie muttered as she marched back to center field.

Margaret lowered a hand to help Jeremy up. "You think you might be able to stay on your feet?"

Jeremy wiped the mud from his legs. "Are my feet still attached?"

"At least we get possession now," Angelina called out from goal.

"We'll see how long that lasts," one of the Troop 224 girls said. Her sash read *Porsche*. Jeremy wondered if it shouldn't say *Mack Truck*.

On the next play, Margaret passed the ball to Ericka, who passed it to Slater. Slater tapped the ball a few times, advancing up the field, and looked up to pass to Jeremy. "See? This isn't so—"

BAM!!!

A red sash steamrolled him from behind. Slater's head snapped back and his stick popped no less than ten feet into the air. Another red sash swooped in, took possession of the ball, and, after a few passes, the score was two to zero. Jeremy rushed over to help Slater up. His entire front was covered in mud.

"Don't laugh," Slater said, groaning. "I have a feeling that this is just the beginning."

And just the beginning it was. The game went on that way, the ogres of Troop 224 leveling the Cadets of 149. Amazingly, when the halftime whistle blew the score was only six to one in favor of Troop 224 (mostly due to some brilliant goaltending on the part of Angelina and a backhanded flick by Margaret worthy of an ESPN highlight reel). However, if you took into account how battered the girls of Troop 149 were, the gap was much larger. They sat panting in a filthy heap on the sideline. It was impossible to distinguish between mud and bruise and muddy bruise.

Ms. Rendell paced around them. "Girls," she said, this time more softly than before. "We need to fight back here. This game is not finished. Those girls are not—"

"Mom," another voice cut in. It came from the top of the bleachers. "Let me handle this."

Jeremy's already tight shoulders tightened up some more. It was Paul. He was wearing his Thomas Scolari Academy for Boys jacket, a pair of shorts, and his soccer shin guards. A bandana was tied around his head, which made him look even meaner.

Ms. Rendell hunkered under her umbrella and stepped aside for her son. Paul pounded down the bleachers, each footfall rattling the aluminum benches.

"Look," he said. "I won't pretend to know the first thing about field hockey—it's a stupid game for girls—but if there's one thing I know, it's how to win." Paul began marching up and down the sideline like he was a general in a bad war movie. "There are two ways to do well in a sport like this: with strength . . ." He peered across the field at the red sashes standing like a brick wall in size order from hulking to monolithic. "Which you probably won't be able to do. But you can also win this game with speed. There is no way they can outrun this!" Paul held up a field hockey ball. *Bip! Bop! Bam!* You've got to pass, girls! Get the ball to your open players. Stick and move." He paused, obviously for dramatic effect. "Isn't that how David beat Goliath?"

One of the smaller girls raised her hand and Paul pointed at her.

"David beat Goliath by hitting him in the head with a rock."

"Whatever," Paul said.

Then he laid out his plan. Jeremy was actually impressed. In the span of minutes, Paul explained the idea of zones and how to cover them, of how to draw defenders from one part of the field to another in order to leave space open for your attackers. He even explained how the other team's larger size would lead to earlier fatigue, giving Troop 149 increased opportunity toward the end of the game.

The end of the game. Jeremy longed for the end of the game. The amazing thing was that with Paul's new strategy, he was beginning to think they had some hope.

Once the girls found their places on the field and the whistle sounded, things began to take a turn for the better. They were passing more often and running Troop 224 around. They were working together and meticulously moving the ball down the field. They worked as a team, eleven foxes outsmarting a bunch of lumbering bears.

Make no mistake, Troop 149 was still taking its share of punishment, but one thing about sports is that once momentum starts turning around sometimes it's hard to stop. The passes went from Margaret to Slater to Ericka to Jeremy. Even some of the smaller, more wiry girls got involved. When tiny Cheryl Cahill heard the tides were changing, she emerged from the bathroom and got into the mix, dealing a wicked hip check to a girl twice her size. The red sash, whose name read

Chelsea, flipped through the air and landed face-first in the deepest muck of the field.

All the while, Angelina called the plays. From her spot at goal she could see the distribution of the red sashes perfectly. She could warn players of coming attacks and she guided them to goal after goal.

With only seconds left in the game, Mrs. Sanchez called for a time-out. The score was tied at twelve and Troop 149's energy was at an all-time high. Not an inch of any player wasn't covered in mud, with the exception of fifteen white smiles.

"Girls," Ms. Rendell said. She was still nearly dry under her umbrella. "You are doing great. Keep doing what you are doing and this game is ours. I'm not going to give you any advice aside from, 'Get back out there and win!'"

The girls cheered, but it sounded more like a fierce battle cry. Each girl clutched her stick and trotted back out onto the field. They took their positions and waited for Troop 224 to take theirs.

Once again, Jeremy was staring across at Sophie, who grinned an evil, gap-toothed grin at him. "This is so over," Sophie growled. She dug her cleats deep into the mud and eyed the ball at center field.

Jeremy looked from side to side and saw that the others could sense something was going to happen, too.

"Ms. Rendell!" Cheryl Cahill called out. "I think I need to go to the bathroom again!"

But it was too late for bathroom breaks. It was too late for anything. The whistle tweeted and all eleven girls from Troop 224, including their goaltender, charged their defenders. They struck hard and then all leaped at the ball at once, like eleven meteors striking a small moon from every different direction. Margaret, who was playing center, was next to the moon and took the brunt of the impact. The girls of Troop 149 dove in to swat the ball out of the scrum and take possession, to resume their strategy and win the game, but that was impossible with the wall of red sashes clustered around.

Jeremy found himself on the outside of the bunch, poking his stick between stomping feet to try and knock the ball free.

"Hit it to me!" Slater cried out. "Their goal is untended!"

"Keep the ball away from them!" another voice cried out.

Jeremy saw the ball flash between someone's knee

and another girl's stick. It disappeared again and he leaned forward to spot it. That's when he caught the elbow to the jaw. Jeremy had never thought it was possible to see stars after getting hit—he'd figured that was only in cartoons—but he came to discover that he'd just never been hit hard enough.

Jeremy fell back and couldn't tell if he was the one spinning or if it was the rest of the world spinning around him. He rubbed his chin and tried to shake it off, but he still felt wobbly. Meanwhile the scrum kept pushing and pulling, tugging and shoving, beside him. Primal screams, grunting and growling, erupted from the knot of girls as they fought to gain possession.

Jeremy heard Ms. Rendell's voice creeping in from the edges. "Jenna! Jenna! Look down!"

It took a moment for Jeremy to remember that *he* was Jenna. It took another moment for him to piece together what she wanted him to do.

He looked down.

Between his streaked-with-mud legs he saw the streaked-with-mud field hockey ball. It was partially buried in the ground, but there was no mistaking it. The girls were struggling next to him for a ball that he had sole possession of.

Jeremy climbed to his feet and Slater trotted up alongside him.

"You ready for this?" Slater asked.

Jeremy nodded.

"Except . . ." Slater pointed at his head. "Your wig's crooked."

Jeremy straightened his wig.

"Better."

Jeremy bent forward and gave the ball a solid *thwack* toward the untended goal. He hurried after it. The ground was so soupy that the ball didn't travel far. He chased it down and swatted it again, this time to Slater, who was running alongside him. *Thwack!*

"Where'd you find the ball?" Slater asked.

"It popped out of the scrum and I fell on it."

Slater hooted with glee and passed the ball back.

Jeremy heard shouting and knew the cluster was breaking up. They were chasing him down. Without a stutter, Jeremy flicked the ball again. This time, it got some air and took a few good bounces before settling down in front of Slater. Slater swatted the ball a few more times before the shouting behind them got too close for his comfort. He passed to Jeremy, who squared up to the untended goal and swung.

It was a perfect shot, one that came from his hips rather than his arms. Jeremy had never had a field hockey lesson in his life. In fact, he hadn't ever held a field hockey stick before today. But he could feel the power of this swing as the rubber ball fired off the face of his stick.

And, just as the final whistle sounded the end of the game, the shot hit dead center, right between the posts into the deepest part of the net.

Jeremy dropped to his knees like he'd seen soccer players do on television. He tossed his stick in the air and let the rain pour down on his face. Slater piled on top of him and they both rolled into the mud. But Jeremy didn't care. He had never won a game at the final buzzer before. In fact, he was usually the last to be picked for any team and rarely on the winning side.

Jeremy took in a deep breath. He wanted to smell the victory, to remember every detail. The trouble was, when he opened his eyes, he saw eleven mud-covered Cadets scowling at him.

Jeremy glanced at the sideline to see the hulking girls of Troop 224 dancing around Mrs. Sanchez, who was pumping her arms in triumph.

He looked to the opposite sideline, where Ms.

Rendell and Paul stood under her umbrella, their heads swinging from side to side.

Jeremy looked back at the girls standing around him, and the one who was clearly Margaret Parsley (Jeremy could tell because it was the pinchiest scowl of the eleven) said, "You scored that goal for the other team."

14

Malicious In Tent

"I'm so sorry, Jenna and Samantha," Ms. Rendell said at Monday's meeting. "With a score for the other team in the final seconds, I'm afraid I can't give either of you a Sports Star Caliber Badge."

"But we played really well in the second half," Slater said. "We worked together. We helped the team and—"

"And you lost the game because you were careless. You didn't have your wits about you and—whether it's on the field hockey field or in real life—that could be a dangerous thing."

Well, you were too busy with your rivalry with

Mrs. Sanchez to offer any help, Jeremy wanted to say, but all that came out was, "Can't you just let it slide?"

None of the girls nodded; none even lifted their eyes.

Ms. Rendell shook her head. "Why don't you try for a different badge?" She grabbed a dry-erase marker and went back to the whiteboard to tally fund-raiser sales. When she finished logging in cupcakes, it was no surprise to anyone that Jenna and Samantha had the worst numbers of the group.

Jeremy looked the girls over. Most of them were sitting, ankles crossed, around the circle. One girl held a Thanksgiving centerpiece she was submitting for her Creative Creations badge. Another held a framed photo of a monarch butterfly she had snagged, tagged, and released for her Wildlife Preservation badge. Each girl had at least three or four badges stitched to her sash. Some had close to a dozen. What were he and Slater doing so wrong that they couldn't earn a single one? What were they doing so wrong that they couldn't sell more than a handful of cupcakes? Jeremy gritted his teeth. The Windjammer Whirl was only a few weeks away and they hadn't even begun to design their balsa wood boat yet.

"Before we hear all about Madeline McEneny's community theater project, why don't we finalize our plans for next weekend's overnight camping trip?" Ms. Rendell said. She began handing out photocopies. "I've listed all the things you will need. A sleeping bag, warm clothing, a flashlight, all that. Then there are a few items we'll need volunteers to bring. Things we can share, such as air mattresses, coolers, garbage bags, et cetera." She handed the last photocopy to the last Cupcake Cadet and took a seat at the head of the circle, near the auditorium stage. "I will take care of the rest. Please do not bring any food, snacks especially. A few of you are on restricted diets and I don't want any calamities. The last thing we need is for Lily Martin to come within fifty feet of a tree nut. We're roughing it, girls. Let's try our best to keep it simple."

Some girl raised her hand. "What about s'mores?"

Ms. Rendell smiled. "Do you think I'm a barbarian? I'll bring all the fixings for s'mores."

A collective sigh came from the group.

"I know it's only October, but nights can get cold up there," Ms. Rendell said. "You'll need to be prepared. Bring sweatshirts and rain gear. Review your handbooks for the proper way to pitch a tent. We'll be going over that later on. There is a Wilderness Survival Caliber Badge in it for each of you."

"Wilderness Survival," Jeremy whispered.

"One third of what we need," Slater said. "There's just one problem."

Jeremy gave him a puzzled look.

Slater held up the photocopy Ms. Rendell had given each of them. He pointed to a sentence printed in bold. Not only was it printed in bold, but it was highlighted by hand in bright yellow.

It said: *Three to a tent. NO EXCEPTIONS!!!*

Fiberglass, Nylon, and Elastic Waistbands

"It says here that fiberglass rod A is supposed to thread through loops one, three, and five." Jeremy flipped through the instructions as Slater struggled with the equipment. The tent looked nothing like the handsome blue-and-gray dome pictured on the manual. Instead the boys were standing around a mess of nylon fabric, plastic stakes, and fiberglass poles.

"Which one is rod A?" Slater asked, sorting through the heap. "I don't see any loops at all. It's all zippers, tabs, and snaps."

Jeremy squinted against the sun glittering on the water and looked around the campsite situated on the edge of Schroon Lake. The autumn air was crisp and smelled of fallen leaves. There wasn't a road or a house or any other signs of civilization. It was perfect for a weekend of campfires, cookouts, hiking, fishing, and boating . . . and Jeremy was excited about all of those things. What did not excite him was the idea of getting caught on a camping trip without his parents' knowledge. The boys had told their folks that each was staying overnight at the other's house. Chance of getting snagged: high. But only those who dared to fail greatly could ever achieve greatly. And as far as dares went, this was a biggie.

The other Cadet teams already had their tents pitched, seven perfect domes, six for the cadets and one for Ms. Rendell and Paul, who, according to him, was only along because his father was at a conference for the weekend.

"Nice tights," Jeremy said.

Slater looked down at his orange-and-white-striped leggings. "I'll be the one laughing when you're freezing your tail off later on. Anyhow, football players wear panty hose."

"They do?" Jeremy asked.

"They used to." Slater fiddled with one of the flexible rods. "How in the world did the other Cadets get their tents up so fast?"

"You two are useless," Margaret Parsley said from behind them. She marched past Jeremy, snatched a pole from Slater's hands, grabbed another from the ground, and snapped the two together end to end. "This," she said, holding the long pole up, "is rod A. Weren't you paying attention at the last meeting?"

"I guess not closely enough," Jeremy said. He held up the nylon fabric. "Did Ms. Rendell mention where loops one, three, and five are?"

Margaret sighed. "You make the loops by snapping down the tabs." She folded one over on itself and pressed the ends together. "There, now you have a loop. Simple."

"Cool," Slater said. "Thanks."

"I'm not helping you," Margaret said. "I'm helping myself." She pointed to her bag, which was leaning against a nearby tree. "Three to a tent and I'm odd girl out."

"Lucky us," Slater muttered.

"I'm not too thrilled about it, either," she said, "but

I made a deal with the other girls. . . ."

"What sort of deal?" Jeremy asked. He tugged down the fabric of his skirt, which was riding up his thighs.

Margaret smiled. "They've agreed to sell the rest of my cupcakes if I bunked with you. Great deal considering no one is selling very many. Anyhow, I've got a new windjammer design and I need to free up my afternoons for time trials."

"Time trials?" Jeremy said.

"The Windjammer Whirl is three weeks away," Slater added. "You've already built your sailboat?"

"Built it? I'm already on my third prototype." Margaret began snapping all the loops on the tent. "I'm having a little trouble with drag on one of my outriggers. It keeps pulling my windjammer to the right."

Jeremy felt a sense of dread wash over him. They hadn't begun to work on their sailboat, they hadn't earned a single badge, and the wagon of unsold cupcakes was still sitting in the icehouse.

"Wow," Jeremy said, handing Margaret another pole. "Sounds like you take this silly little boat race seriously."

"This is *not* a silly little boat race," she said. "It's a

matter of troop pride. I've won first place three years straight and I plan to make this my fourth. No Cadet has ever won four in a row. Those girls from Troop 224 might crush us at field hockey, but we rule the Windjammer Whirl. That online aerodynamics class wasn't for nothing."

Outriggers? Aerodynamics? Three prototypes? Jeremy had seen the windjammer kit in the Cupcake Cadet manual. It contained a block of balsa wood, a dowel for the mast, and a plastic sail. He figured all he'd have to do is slap the thing together and paint it, winning by the sheer force of his and Slater's genetically bigger boy lungs. *Where did she get an outrigger? What* was *an outrigger?*

Margaret showed the boys, step by step, how to pitch the tent. All the while she described the innovations she had planned for her windjammer. "A flatter bottom allows the vessel to turn more easily, but make it too flat and it spins when you blow into the sails. Here, slide this rod through those loops. No, loops B, D, and F. I'm also adding a number of side sails for easier steering. . . ."

The boys did as Margaret instructed—sliding rods through loops, zipping zippers, and snapping snaps—

all the while listening to their chances of winning the Windjammer Whirl slip away. Suddenly, the tent popped to life. Jeremy was amazed at how easily Margaret had done everything. Sure, she had been a Cupcake Cadet for a few years now, but something like pitching a tent was supposed to be easy.

Ms. Rendell strolled over with Paul not far behind. "How are things going over here, ladies?" she asked.

"Fine," Jeremy said, tugging the air pump from Slater's hands. "Just getting this air mattress inflated."

Slater snatched the pump back. "Actually, *I* was getting the mattress inflated."

"Girls, this is a team effort." Ms. Rendell made some marks on her clipboard. "Either the three of you get badges or none of you do. Let's try to work together."

Paul took the air pump from Jeremy. He placed it on the ground and started stomping on it. "It's faster if you do it like this."

"Uh, thanks," Jeremy said.

Paul grinned. "No problem."

Ms. Rendell walked along to inspect another tent, but Paul lingered behind. "Did you bring the goods?" he asked Slater. "I'd hate to see your boyfriends shoved in their lockers on Monday morning."

Slater unzipped Jeremy's backpack and produced five cupcakes. "Five for five dollars," he said. Cash changed hands and Paul went on his way.

Margaret turned on the boys. "What was that all about?"

"Just a business deal we've got going," Jeremy said.

"What sort of business deal?"

"Wouldn't you like to know?" Slater said.

"Paul is on a strict diet," Margaret said. "His mom brings him to these meetings so she can keep an eye on what he eats."

"So?" Jeremy said.

"So," Margaret snapped back, "if Ms. Rendell sees you stuffing her son full of cupcakes she is going to get M . . . A . . . D . . . mad."

Slater grinned. "Only those who dare to fail greatly can ever achieve greatly."

"Well, you two are pretty good at the failing part," Margaret said. "If you guys blow my chances at an Wilderness Survival badge, I'm going to make your lives miserable. Now, Samantha, get pumping while Jenna and I load the bags into the tent."

Margaret crawled into the blue dome as Jeremy gathered their backpacks.

"Come on!" Margaret insisted, her hand shooting out between the tent flaps. "We don't have all afternoon."

Jeremy grabbed his bag and handed it to Margaret. Then he handed her Slater's. Although he felt like hurling Margaret's into the lake, he pushed it into the tent after the other two. The trouble was that Margaret didn't take it. He shook the backpack. "Are you going to take this bag or should I just chuck it in there?" Jeremy asked.

Silence.

"Margaret?" Jeremy shook the backpack again. "Is everything okay?"

He heard some rustling, then some murmuring, and Jeremy sensed that everything was not okay. He bent down to stick his head inside, but as he did he almost cracked skulls with Margaret. She scrambled from the tent like there was an open crate of scorpions in there. She glared at Jeremy, then at Slater. "Who are . . . ?"

But before she found the words to finish her sentence, she raced off.

"What was that all about?" Slater asked, his foot hovering over the pump.

Jeremy ducked into the tent to see what had spooked

her. The backpacks were lined up neatly against the rear wall. His bag was partially unzipped from when Slater had fished out Paul's cupcakes. He could see a few of his T-shirts and the sleeve of his fleece, but other than that everything seemed in place. Then, on the far side of the tent, deep in the shadowy corner, Jeremy could make out a crumpled mass. He crawled over to get a better look. It was a balled-up piece of white cloth. Jeremy peered closer and saw a familiar elastic waistband with a tag sewn in. It was the same tag Jeremy's mother sewed in all of his clothing. In bold lettering it read: *JEREMY*. He picked up the cloth by the tag and his heart began to pound.

"What's up with Margaret?" Slater asked from outside. "Did she a ghost or something?"

"Worse," Jeremy said, crawling from the tent. He stood up and straightened his wig. "She saw my underwear."

The Trouble with Tighty-Whities

"*Y*ou two had better start explaining," Margaret said after several minutes thinking things over under a huge spruce tree. "Otherwise, I'm going straight to the other girls. I'll go to Ms. Rendell. I might just go straight to the Cupcake Cadet high council!"

"The Cupcake Cadets have a high council?" Slater asked.

"It's in Missoula, Montana," Jeremy said. "Page twelve of the *Cupcake Cadet Handbook*."

"Weird."

"It's not weird, and you would know all about it if you read the thing once in a while." Margaret shook her head and scowled. "I guess it won't make much difference since you're both turning in your sashes today."

"Today?!" the boys cried out.

"That's right," Margaret said. "You two are going to turn in your sashes and tell Ms. Rendell what you've been up to in front of the whole troop. It'll make my s'mores all the more tasty."

"Just settle down," Jeremy said.

"Don't tell me to settle down!" Margaret was pacing back and forth now like a lion in a too-small cage. "You are flouting our organization."

"I don't even know what *flouting* means," Slater muttered.

"It means you're making a mockery of what Cupcake Cadets do."

Slater's shoulders sagged. "Oh, that."

"Let us explain," Jeremy said.

"Explain?" Margaret stepped right up to him until they were nose-to-nose. "Both of you are in direct violation of Rule B101-A2, Section Four of the Cupcake Cadet Code of Conduct: No boys! Not to mention you lied to every one of us."

A few girls from a nearby tent looked over.

"Please," Jeremy said. "Hear us out—"

"What could you possibly say to make me think what you're doing is okay?" By now her arms were flailing and her voice was shaking the branches of nearby trees.

"Just give us a chance." Jeremy gave Margaret the look he used on his mom when he wanted to get out of some kind of trouble.

Margaret did not soften, but she glanced at her watch. "I'll give you thirty seconds, and when I say thirty I mean it. If you take thirty-one, I'm screaming bloody murder."

"Deal."

Jeremy led Margaret into the tent and tucked his underwear out of sight. Slater sat next to him.

Margaret glanced at her watch, then looked at them expectantly.

Slater was the first to speak. "I told Jeremy that this would never work, that—"

Margaret lifted a hand to silence him. "Why are you here?" she said. "What made you guys think it would be a good idea to dress as Cadets and join the troop?"

As quickly and as clearly as he could, Jeremy told Margaret about their plan. He told her about the damage to his father's boat and how they had until spring to repair it. He told her about seeing the poster at the library and finding the uniforms in the icehouse. He told her how he and Slater figured it would be easy to win the Windjammer Whirl. Then, he told her how wrong they had been.

By the time Jeremy finished, it had been more than thirty seconds. It had been closer to five minutes. Margaret hadn't gone running from the tent. She just sat there, a grim, unmoving expression on her face, like she was a judge deciding someone's sentence in a court case, which, when Jeremy thought about it, she sort of was.

Finally, she spoke. "I can't believe I didn't see it sooner," she said. "I thought the two of you were really stupid, incompetent girls. Now I can see you're just boys."

Jeremy didn't say anything to defend his gender. It would only push Margaret away; he wanted to draw her closer. "Come on," he said. "Has it been that bad these past couple of weeks?"

"Honestly?" Margaret said.

"Honestly."

"It's been terrible. We had to eat that disgusting pie and you blew the field hockey game for us. Worst of all, you've been marching all around town making a big joke out of what a lot of us take really seriously."

"But now we see how hard it is to be Cadets." Slater pulled off his tam and met Margaret's glare with his goofy grin. "That has to count for something."

Margaret was about to say something back, but someone tapped on the outside of the tent. "Is everything okay?" It was Paul. "Lots of work to do out here!" he said cheerfully.

Jeremy's eyes darted to Margaret. If she wanted to, she could destroy them. It was one thing to quietly quit the Cupcake Cadets once they got home; it was another to be ratted out deep in the woods at the beginning of their weekend-long camping trip. What would happen? Would they be banished from the site, forced to camp somewhere else? Would Ms. Rendell pack up the troop and bring everyone home? Would the girls use some extra rope to hang them upside down from tree limbs until it was time to head out? Right now, Margaret had all the power—Jeremy figured that was the way she liked it—and the best he could do was mouth a single word:

Please.

Paul poked his head into the tent. "Sorry to bother you, but my mom wants to make sure the campsite is finished. We've got to gather more kindling, clear the path to the bathroom, and a few other things. She wants to get down to the water ASAP but not until the work here is done."

"We'll be out in just a minute," Margaret said. "We're just figuring out sleeping arrangements."

"Okeley-dokeley," he said and disappeared.

Okeley-dokeley?

When they heard Paul's distant voice directing someone else how to store the food so wild animals wouldn't get to it, Jeremy exhaled. "Thanks, Margaret," he said.

"Yeah, thanks," Slater said.

"Don't thank me yet," Margaret said. "By the time we're done, I think you'll wish I *had* blown your cover. It's going to be fun to prove how incompetent boys really are." She pulled out her cell phone. "Now squeeze together so I can get a photo of you."

"A photo?" Slater said. "What do you need a photo for?"

Margaret peered at the screen of her cell phone.

"For insurance, of course. I can't have you going home and hanging up your skirts forever."

Slater slapped on his tam and the boys moved next to each other as Margaret lined up the picture.

"One thing you need to remember about being a girl, though . . ." she said.

"What's that?" Jeremy asked.

"Cross your legs."

"Huh?"

"I said cross your legs." Margaret smiled. "You don't want the camera to see up your—"

Click!

Making a Splash

Although she said it was against every shred of Cupcake Cadet loyalty in her body, Margaret agreed to keep the boys' secret. She even agreed to let them participate in the Windjammer Whirl. But Margaret had a few conditions.

First, she wanted any and all money the boys had already collected for the fund-raiser. She agreed to give them her unsold cupcakes in exchange for the money, but any sales they had already made were hers. They could start from scratch.

Second, if the boys somehow managed to win the Windjammer Whirl, which she seriously doubted,

Margaret would get half the prize money. The boys argued that they could just leave the Cadets after the weekend, but Margaret waggled her phone and told them that they had better stick with the plan or that photo would find its way onto the internet. Or better yet, into the newspaper.

They were trapped.

The boys were sitting on the dock, heads hanging, when Ms. Rendell walked up behind them. "What's the trouble, ladies?"

"Just enjoying the lake," Jeremy said.

Slater skipped a stone across the still water. It bounced four or five times, then plopped below the surface. "You know, taking in nature like a good Cupcake Cadet should."

"Nice sidearm." Ms. Rendell lowered herself between Jeremy and Slater and sat on the edge of the dock. "It's about the badges, isn't it?"

A Caliber Badge was the furthest thing from Jeremy's mind. Even if they got all three, even if they sold all their cupcakes, and even if they somehow found the time to design a winning windjammer, they'd still have to give half of the five-hundred-dollar prize to Margaret. That left only two hundred and fifty for them, not nearly enough to fix the boat.

Slater poked a stick into a small hole in his purple polka-dot leggings. "The Sailboat Serenade is only a few weeks away and—"

"Windjammer Whirl," Jeremy said.

"Whatever," Slater said. "The race is only a few weeks away and we're batting a big fat zero."

"It's not for lack of trying," Ms. Rendell said, "but being a Cupcake Cadet means more than just squeaking by. Effort is important, of course, but being successful means getting results. It's impossible to make the perfect cupcake unless you measure the ingredients carefully and bring the oven to the right temperature. It also depends on the baking pan you use and the type of frosting. Then there are the sprinkles." She smiled at them. "But this camping trip can provide all sorts of opportunities."

"It can?" Slater said.

"Why, right off the top of my head, I can think of three badges you could earn this weekend. The two of you could make a huge splash." She began looking around the campsite. "There's the Outdoor Adventure badge, but there's also Boating Skills and Plant Identification."

Jeremy looked around. "There's also Orienteering and Fishing Frenzy. I saw those in the handbook."

Ms. Rendell smiled. "Let's start simple," she said.

"The last thing we need is to have you take someone's eye out with a fishhook."

"You make it sound like you have no confidence in us."

Ms. Rendell patted Jeremy on the shoulder. "Sometimes the best recipes are the simple ones."

With only a few adjustments, the bright orange safety vests fit the boys fine. In no time they were ready to set out on the lake in the outboard. Jeremy kept his nose buried in the *Cupcake Cadet Handbook*, making sure he did not miss one of the twelve-point boating safety checks outlined in it. He read them off to Slater:

"No water in the bottom of the boat?"

"Check."

"Bailing cup?"

"Check."

"Flotation devices?"

"Check."

"Anchor and line?"

"Check."

And on they went. Ms. Rendell watched approvingly from the creaky dock along with no less than fifteen of the Cadets. Angelina and Margaret were prepping the canoe while the others were waiting to see how

Jeremy and Slater were going to screw things up this time. Jeremy thought he could hear a few of the girls taking bets on it, but he was confident there would be no catastrophes. After all, he had grown up on the water. He boated with his father all the time.

As Jeremy fiddled with the engine, Slater untied the lines from the dock posts. Although Jeremy was used to a keystart, this outboard wasn't much different from his father's lawn mower. After countless afternoons of doing the lawn, Jeremy was well acquainted with pullstarts. He pressed the primer button several times and began tugging on the starter cord. The engine chug, chug, chugged, then coughed out a cloud of blue smoke. Then it sputtered out.

"Try again," Ms. Rendell called out.

"It's burning oil!" Paul shouted. "Looks like you primed it too much."

Jeremy went back to tugging. More blue smoke coughed out.

"Dude, let me give it a whirl," Slater said. "I've got the magic touch."

Slater pulled the cord hard.

"That's the spirit!" Ms. Rendell yelled.

Slater yanked on the cord again and tumbled backward. The engine coughed twice, then struggled to life. Ms. Rendell and then the Cadets began cheering them on. The dock creaked every time someone's hiking boots came down on the old wooden slats.

"I should drive," Jeremy said. "I have more boating experience."

"Maybe we both should drive," Slater said. "I have the magic touch."

The boys perched themselves triumphantly on the back edge of the boat and each put a hand on the throttle. Together, they lowered the propeller into the water. Jeremy couldn't help but smile at the sight of Slater next to him, at the helm of a boat in full Cupcake Cadet uniform. His orange-and-white tights bunched up around the tops of his sneakers.

As they made their way into the deeper water, Jeremy drew in a breath. They were boating. They were boating in a real boat on a real lake with no adults on board. If his father could see him now, he would have no problem tossing over the keys to the Chris-Craft.

Jeremy waved over his shoulder at Ms. Rendell. She seemed to be jumping around, her arms pumping over her head. So were the other girls. Were they cheering? He couldn't hear over the puttering of the engine. Was that a look of concern on Ms. Rendell's face? Was that Paul frantically untying something from the dock?

Suddenly, a rope went taut and snapped out of the water behind them. The tension in the line stopped the boat dead. Jeremy fell from the bench and his gaze landed on an eyehook at the stern. There was a rope tied to it that made a straight line to the endpost of the rickety dock. Ms. Rendell and the girls stumbled, several of them almost falling into the water.

"What the . . . ?" Slater said. He swatted the side of the engine with an open palm and hit the throttle. The bow of the boat rose out of the water and the engine strained with a high-pitched whine.

The endpost buckled a little, then began to pull free of the dock. "That's more like it," Slater said as the failing post gave them some slack. "Must be a problem with the prop or something."

"Whoa!" Jeremy cried out.

"Whoa is right, dude!" Slater gave the throttle another squeeze and the engine screamed louder. The bow rose higher into the air as water churned and bubbled behind the boat.

"No, I mean . . ."

"You mean wh—?"

The endpost gave way with a splintering crack. Ms. Rendell, Paul, and the Cadets scrambled to reach solid ground before the entire dock pulled away from the shore. One by one, girls dropped into the water as the dock collapsed into the lake. Another crack split the air as a second post snapped. It didn't take much more for the last bits of wood to give way and for the last of the Cupcake Cadets to plummet into the water. Ms. Rendell's arms flailed like a wobbly surfer's, but she had nothing to hold on to except Paul. Their plunge into the water made the biggest splash of all.

"We're making some headway now!" Slater cried out, still unaware of what was going on behind him.

Jeremy watched Slater destroy the dock along with any chance they might have had at scoring a Caliber Badge. He watched as the Cadets splashed and fumbled in the cold water, groping their way to shore.

Finally Slater turned around. His hand came off the throttle and the boat settled into the water, bobbing innocently as though it hadn't just wreaked complete havoc. Slater's victorious grin turned into a look of horror.

Margaret Parsley seemed to be the only dry person in the bunch. She glared at them from shore with her arms folded and shook her head in disappointment.

Pow-Wow Now

Ms. Rendell, Paul, and all the Cupcake Cadets sat in a circle around the fire pit. A fire popped and crackled and all of the soaked-through Cadets huddled around to warm themselves. All of the Cadets, that is, except Jeremy and Slater, who sat on a log near the minibus. Everyone was silent, the only communication being scowls, frowns, and evil stares. Although it was sunny, the good weather was not enough to take away the cloud that had settled over the Cupcake Cadet campout.

"I'm sorry," Ms. Rendell said to the troop. "It looks like we're going to have to pack up."

The girls let out a collective moan.

"We can't go," Angelina protested. A few of the others nodded in agreement. "If we put it off any longer, it'll be too cold to do an overnight. This is the highlight of the season!"

"What about the Windjammer Whirl?" Margaret said.

"The Windjammer Whirl is the highlight of *your* season," Angelina said. "The highlight of *our* season is the camping trip."

"I'm afraid we have no choice," Ms. Rendell said, looking around the ring of dripping wet girls. "It's too chilly to sleep in wet clothes, and not all of you have extra sweatshirts and fleeces. Anyhow, the dock is destroyed and we had twenty near-injuries. It's going to take me a week just to fill out the accident reports and explain to all your parents."

Jeremy tried to avoid Margaret's stare but he could feel it burning twin holes in the side of his face. In fact, Jeremy could feel the heated stares of all the Cupcake Cadets. He was surprised he hadn't already burst into flames.

Angelina stood and planted her fists on her hips. "But isn't being a Cupcake Cadet all about working together? Isn't it about coming up with solutions to problems, about thinking outside of the carton?"

Ms. Rendell nodded, but it was one of those I-agree-with-you-but-I-can't-say-yes nods. "That's true, Angelina, but—"

Ericka stood alongside Angelina. "Isn't Cupcake Cadets all about proving that girls are capable of anything?" A few girls began murmuring in agreement.

"I appreciate that you've all been memorizing your handbooks, but considering what happened, considering that we've caused so much damage to the campsite, I can't imagine your parents would want us to stay."

Margaret stood next to Ericka. "And isn't it about proving we're capable of doing anything we set our minds to, even if a few stupid boys screw it all up?"

Jeremy's stomach lurched like it was filled with a hundred squirming eels. He felt Slater tense up, too.

"What does any of this have to do with boys?" Ms. Rendell asked.

Margaret eyed Jeremy and Slater and her lips tightened. Jeremy could see her jaw muscles clenching over and over like the words were struggling to burst right out of her mouth.

"Nothing, I guess. I'm just saying if this were an

all-boys campout, they'd turn tail and run home. We're girls and we're tough. We need to stick it out. It's no different than what the pioneers had to do."

Ms. Rendell looked around the circle at the girls, all of whom were nodding in agreement.

"Why don't we take a vote?" Angelina suggested. "A vote would be fair."

Excitement swelled as the girls began to fall into agreement. After a few nudges, even the reluctant ones started pumping their fists and clamoring for Ms. Rendell to give the okay. Sure, it would mean lots of extra work. Sure, it would mean sharing clothing and having some of them sleep in the bus. But they were Cupcake Cadets, and Cupcake Cadets never ran away from a challenge.

Before long, the girls were all standing around the campfire, their arms locked. They began to chant: *"Let us stay! Let us stay! Let us stay!"*

Then Slater got up.

"What are you doing?" Jeremy hissed at him.

Slater leaned in close. "If Rendell lets us stay it won't be nearly as bad. Riding an hour and a half home after destroying their campout would be like giving raw meat to a pack of wild dogs. Things'll smooth out overnight."

Slater had a point. Jeremy stood and began chanting in sync with the others.

"Let us stay! Let us stay! Let us stay!"

He linked his arm with Ericka's. She looked up at him and scowled, then turned back to chanting.

Finally, Ms. Rendell lifted her hand and smiled. Jeremy was sure she was going to give in, but once she stood her expression turned sad. "I'm afraid not, ladies. This is one time where I'm going to have to make a decision for the group. Let's pack up and head home."

The eels in Jeremy's stomach began to squirm even more. His hands shook as he broke down the tent and packed his bag. His legs wobbled as they carried him onto the bus. He and Slater slid into the first row while the rest of the Cadets moved as far back as possible. Despite every song Ms. Rendell tried to sing, the wall of silence didn't crumble. In fact, the wall of silence didn't even get a hairline crack. Jeremy guessed that teamwork, cooperation, innovative thinking, and a little vanilla frosting—all the things that made a good Cupcake Cadet—only went so far.

Bobby Kennedy to the Rescue!

"What's the point of building this stupid thing?" Slater asked, tossing the windjammer box across the desktop.

"You can't win a model boat race without a model boat," Jeremy said.

"Dude, we can't *enter* the model boat race without selling our cupcakes, and we're back to square one."

"We'll think of something," Jeremy said. "But if we have nothing to race then this whole thing was for nothing. I am not okay with that."

"I am not okay with any of this!" Slater said. "It's not just the cupcakes. We still need three Caliber

Badges." He grabbed his new issue of *Rad-Sk8r* and began flipping through the pages. "Margaret took an aerodynamics class! Who takes a class to win a model boat race?"

Jeremy stared at his father's boat on the trailer. It was covered with bright blue plastic tarp. He knew if he were to lift that tarp he would see the damage he had done. And that would remind him of the money it would cost to get it fixed.

Jeremy held up the model sailboat box. "Let's keep our eyes on the prize."

"Dude, there is no prize. All of this was for nothing. It was for less than nothing."

"We just have to think about this problem in a new way."

"Begging Margaret for mercy is a good start."

Jeremy shook his head. "That will only give her the power she wants. She'll know she has sway over us." He ran his palm along the hull of his father's boat. It felt cold, rigid, and smooth. "Remember that first day we put on the uniforms? Remember how tough it was to come out from behind the boat? You hid back there for twenty minutes before you even peeked out."

"It wasn't twenty minutes," Slater said.

"Then remember how nervous you were walking through the woods on our way to our first meeting?"

Slater reluctantly nodded.

Jeremy took Slater's magazine and tossed it on the desk. He poked Slater's chest. "What was it that you told me? 'Only those who dare to fail greatly . . .'"

Slater sighed and finished the quote. "'. . . can ever achieve greatly.'"

"That's right."

"So, what do you think we should do?" Slater asked.

Jeremy held up the model windjammer box again. "I think we should sell all our cupcakes, get our three Caliber Badges, and build this stupid little boat. Then, we should win the Windjammer Whirl."

"Fat chance," Slater said.

Jeremy fished the instructions out of the box, spread them out on the desk, and dropped into the office chair. "It's better than a skinny chance."

The boys huddled over the instructions together and read:

```
┌─────────────────────────────────────────────────┐
│                                                   │
│            WINDJAMMER INSTRUCTIONS                │
│   Thank you for your interest in the Cupcake Cadet │
│     Windjammer Whirl. The good people at the home  │
│    office in Missoula, Montana, thought this friendly │
│   competition would help reinforce the ideals the  │
│  Cupcake Cadets were built upon: teamwork, innovative │
│     thinking, and a little vanilla frosting.       │
│                 GOOD LUCK!!                        │
│                                                   │
└─────────────────────────────────────────────────┘
```

"What kind of stupid, worthless instructions are these?" Slater cried out.

Jeremy read the paper again in the hope of gleaning some useful tip. He turned the sheet over and looked at the back. It was blank.

"Any brilliant ideas?" Slater asked.

Jeremy let the instructions slip from his fingers. This time he couldn't feel a single wrinkle working its way into his brain. He couldn't think of one stupid, worthless thing. What did he know about model sailboats? What did he know about the Windjammer Whirl?

It was time for an expert opinion.

164

To the Library!

Ms. Morrison propped her feet on the lower shelf of the book cart. Her fuzzy rainbow socks looked like twin puppets. "What do I know about windjammers?" she said. "I'm just a children's librarian. Anyhow, I've got troubles of my own."

"What sort of trouble does a children's librarian have?" Slater asked. "Isn't it all cats wearing hats and boy wizards with facial scars?"

Jeremy hung back and let Slater do the talking. He still felt awkward after getting his arm stuck in the return chute the previous week. Jeremy had accidentally slipped one of Ruthie's DVDs into the slot. Fearing a monkey scrub, he had reached in to retrieve it. It took three librarians and a half bottle of lotion to free him, and not before Ruthie's DVD, a Beethoven boxed set, and a brand-new copy of *The Guinness Book of World Records* got covered in DermaSoft Skin-So-Smooth. Fortunately, they freed Jeremy before they had to call in the fire department to bring the Jaws of Life.

Ms. Morrison sighed. "Teen karaoke night went a little loud last night and now the reference librarians are all up in my grille. Not only did they interrupt a duet I was doing with our guest author, but they lodged a complaint with the library board."

"Are you kidding me?" Slater pushed his hair out of his eyes and leaned against her desk. "Those reference librarians are totally lame. Isn't this a *media* center? Shouldn't they be cool with all sorts of media?" Ms. Morrison might as well have been a toasted bagel because Slater was buttering her up big-time.

She flipped her blue hair to the side and nodded. "That's what I said."

"And isn't music technically media?"

"That's what I said!" Ms. Morrison perked up in her chair, but then slouched again. "Unfortunately, the reference librarians don't see things the same way we do." She held up a sheet of paper. "I've already gotten a memo from the board. I have to convince them of the value of social events for teens in the library and propose solutions to the noise issue." Ms. Morrison's eyes scanned the paper for a moment. Then she looked at the boys and a smile spread across her face. "So, why do you need to know about model windjammers? Isn't that a Cupcake Cadet thing?"

"I . . . uh . . . we . . . uh . . ."

"You'd better not be messing with the Cupcake Cadets." Ms. Morrison pulled down the collar of her purple sweater to reveal a pin on her shirt. It was a gold cupcake with pink frosting. "I'm a Bountiful Baker, third degree."

"We're not messing with anybody," Jeremy said.

"Ooh, Jeremy, I didn't see you there. How's your arm?"

Jeremy rubbed his shoulder. It was still sore. "Fine."

"What's wrong with your arm?" Slater asked.

"Nothing." Jeremy hadn't told Slater about the arm-in-the-return-slot incident and he didn't want to. He changed the subject back to the matter at hand. "Some girl at the park was bragging about her model windjammer. We bet her we could make a better one."

"And . . . ?"

"And we have no idea what to do," Slater said.

"Don't underestimate the Cupcake Cadets," Ms. Morrison said. "Those girls are ruthless."

The word *ruthless* brought Jeremy's sister, Ruthie, to mind. "Don't we know it," he said.

Ms. Morrison spun her chair to face her computer terminal. "My last year in the Cadets was the first year of the Windjammer Whirl. Boats today are far more advanced than anything we ever did. But I like a challenge. Let's do a keyword search." She began pecking words into the online catalog. "Let's see here . . . Windbreakers . . . wind tunnels . . . breaking wind . . . windup toys . . . Here it is: windjammers. We have six books on the topic."

"Great!" Jeremy said. "Where are they?"

Ms. Morrison ran her finger across the screen. "Hmmmm . . ."

"Hmmmm what?" Slater said. "That didn't sound like a good hmmmm."

Ms. Morrison leaned back in her chair. It squeaked beneath her. "It seems all of our windjammer books have been checked out."

"Checked out?" Jeremy said. "By who?"

"That's a privacy issue," Ms. Morrison said. "I'm not allowed to tell you."

"Come on," Slater pleaded. "We're, like, your best customers. Do you call people at the library customers?"

"We call them patrons."

"Okay, then we're, like, your best patrons."

"Ha!" she said. "You two are *not* my best patrons."

"Well, we're your favorite patrons," Jeremy said. "Plus, we've been coming since we were in diapers. You've known us since we were checking out picture books about pigeons who want to drive mass transit!"

Ms. Morrison grinned. "That poor pigeon never does get to drive that bus." Ms. Morrison tapped a few more keys on her keyboard. "Well, I can't tell you who has the book exactly," she said. "But I *can* give you a hint."

The boys leaned in close.

"Her initials are M.P."

Jeremy and Slater looked at each other. "Margaret Parsley," they said at once.

"Sorry, guys," Ms. Morrison said, propping her feet back on the shelving cart. Her rainbow toes wiggled. "Wish I could help you more."

"Don't sweat it," Jeremy said. "We just need to get a little more ruthless."

The Ruthie-Tania

"Ruuuuuthie?" Jeremy called out as he made his way down the hallway toward his sister's room. Giving her some notice that he was about to interrupt her operation usually softened her up. *Usually.* He could hear Ruthie's fingers working furiously over the keyboard. As he got closer, he began to hear her voice. She sounded both frantic and deeply occupied.

"Are you serious? . . . That's amazing. . . . So, do you like him or do you *like* like him? . . . Did he say anything back? . . . What did you do next?"

Jeremy inched closer until he was peering through her doorway. He knuckled the frame before she could accuse him of eavesdropping. In Ruthie's eyes, there was nothing worse than a no-good, dirty, low-down eavesdropper.

"What do you want?" Ruthie asked without taking her eyes off her monitor. "I'm in the middle of something."

"You should get a headset," Jeremy suggested. "You're going to hurt your neck holding the phone between your ear and shoulder like that. I read an article—"

Ruthie glared at him, then dropped her eyes back to the screen. "I'll put it on my Christmas list. Do you need something or are you just here to make my life miserable?" She grabbed the phone from her shoulder and spoke into it. "No, I'm not talking to you, Brogan. I'm talking to my brother, who was just on his way back under the rock he crawled out from."

Jeremy decided to get right to the point. "I have one question."

Her fingers flew over the keys with more fervor. "Make it quick. It's a busy night."

"They're all busy nights," Jeremy said.

"Gossip doesn't sleep."

Jeremy looked at his feet and began to turn around. "You never have time for me anymore." Jeremy was hoping to tug at Ruthie's heartstrings with that one. That is, if she had heartstrings.

"Maybe it's because you're a major pain," Ruthie

said. "Now tell me what you need or get lost."

Jeremy spun back around, a grin across his face. "I need to find out how to build a model windjammer."

Ruthie's keyboarding stopped. She swiveled in her desk chair to face him. "What did you say?"

"A model windjammer. You know, like the kind they race in the—"

"Cupcake Cadets," Ruthie said suspiciously. "I know what it is." She turned her attention to the phone. "No, Brogan, I'm not still in the Cupcake Cadets. I told you I'm talking to my brother. . . . No, he's not in the . . . Look, I'll call you back, okay?" She turned off the phone and tossed it on her bed.

"I know what the Windjammer Whirl is, Jeremy. I'm just wondering why *you* care about it."

Jeremy hadn't prepared to answer that question. He figured Ruthie would be so wrapped up with her texting and emailing and phone conversations that she would just give him the information he needed and send him on his way. "I need it to help a friend, a girl I know."

"Now we're talking." Ruthie slid to the edge of her chair and leaned even closer. "Who is this girl? Do I know her? Where did you meet her?"

"That's not important. All I need to know is—"

"The details are always important, Jeremy." She

motioned for him to sit on her bed. "I have information you want and you have information I want. That's how this works. Now comes the hard part. You need your information more than I need mine. That means you have to spill the beans first and tell me as much as I want to know or you get a big fat goose egg."

"There are no beans to spill," he said.

"There are always beans to spill," Ruthie said. "You might not realize it, but there are. So, dish." She planted her elbows on her knees and stared at him.

Beans? Geese? Dishes? Jeremy could hardly believe he and this girl sitting across from him came from the same parents. Looking at her he could see their resemblance, but something about her . . . she was just wired differently.

"I don't know," he said. His brain scrambled to think of something to tell her. Something convincing. Finally, he blurted out the first person in his mind. "Her name is Samantha. I know her from the park. She's having trouble with her windjammer and I thought you might have some advice."

Ruthie's nose wrinkled. "Samantha? Not the same Samantha who . . ."

Jeremy's shoulders hunched. "Who what?"

"I'm not sure," Ruthie said. "I heard something a

few weeks ago about the Cupcake Cadets. Something about these new girls."

Jeremy's stomach flipped. "What did you hear?"

"I don't remember everything—Cadet gossip isn't high on my list these days—but Marjorie told me that her sister, Katie, told her there were these new girls in the troop. She said they were the worst, like they were doing everything they could to sabotage them."

"I don't know anything about that," Jeremy said. He stood to go. "Like I said, I just know her from the park. But if you're too busy . . ."

Ruthie flipped her thumb over her shoulder, gesturing to the top shelf of her closet. "My old boat is up there. If you can find it, you're welcome to have it."

"Really?" Jeremy leaped up. It was the nicest thing his sister had ever done for him and the only good thing that had happened in the past few weeks.

"Just keep your hands and eyes off everything else. If a single hair clip is out of place . . ." Ruthie cracked her knuckles. "Let's just say the penalty will be severe."

Jeremy stood on an overturned milk crate and reached into Ruthie's closet. He pushed aside stacks of books and journals, a pile of sweaters, and several hats. He dug deeper and saw a triangular sail poking up from behind a storage basket. He carefully lifted out the small pink boat and inspected it. It had sleek lines and, even after sitting in the dusty closet for so long, still gleamed. The word *RUTHLESS* was printed along the sides in perfect block letters. He could already see this boat cutting through the still water of the kiddie pool, weaving in and out of the obstacles faster than a border collie in an agility competition. Sure, the mast had a hairline crack and the keel was slightly bent, but those were easy fixes. All of a sudden, getting ready for this race seemed easy.

"And while you're in the closet let me know if you find my Cindi Sizzle wig," Ruthie said. "I've been looking for it for weeks and it still hasn't turned up."

Jeremy froze. Then he turned to find Ruthie staring at him.

He looked down at the windjammer and turned it over. His hands began to shake.

He looked back at Ruthie.

She was still staring.

"You've got a lot of explaining to do, *Jenna* Bender."

22

'Fessing Up

Jeremy led his sister out to the icehouse, where Slater was waiting. Ruthie's arms were folded over her chest and she wore an expression that was a mix of anger, concern, and curiosity. But mostly it was that first one.

And an angry Ruthie was a dangerous Ruthie.

"It just sort of happened," Jeremy said, fidgeting with Ruthie's windjammer.

"This sort of thing doesn't just sort of happen," she said.

"Yeah, it does," Slater said. "One day we were all-American boys. You know, catching frogs, skateboarding, and getting into trouble. The next day—"

"The next day you were all-American girls?" Ruthie dropped into the desk chair. "Dressing up as girls and joining the Cupcake Cadets doesn't *just sort of happen*. It's wrong for so many reasons, not the least of which is my reputation. Do you realize what is going to happen to me when people find out what you're doing?"

"People are not going to find out," Jeremy said.

"Of course they are!" she hollered.

Slater began fiddling with the edge of the boat tarp. "It's all Jeremy's fault."

"My fault?" Jeremy cried out.

"Well, it isn't *my* fault!"

Jeremy pointed an accusing finger at Slater. "Who added all those weird ingredients to the apple pie?"

Slater's face turned the color of an overripe tomato. "Who shot the winning goal for the other team?"

"You helped!"

"Well, who left his stupid underwear lying around the tent for Margaret to find? If it wasn't for your tighty-whities, we wouldn't be in this mess!"

Jeremy couldn't say anything to that. It was true. His underwear had been the culprit.

"Look," Ruthie said. "It does no good to argue over whose fault this is. The truth is that you're both idiots.

What made you think a prank like this would work?"

Jeremy leaned against his father's boat and sighed. "We thought we'd be able to win this thing easy. You know, wear the uniform, build a model boat, win the race, make five hundred bucks. It's a bunch of girls. How hard could it be?"

"That was your first mistake," Ruthie said. "Cupcake Cadets might seem like a hokey organization. Cupcakes, all the old-fashioned baking references, the corny outfits. That's because the group was started by a bunch of Betty Crocker homemakers." She leaned back in her chair and shook her head. "It's changed over the years, the Cupcake Cadets. Those daughters grew up and entered the workforce. They changed Cadetting to something different. The next generation changed it more." Ruthie's eyes narrowed. "Sure, they might have kept some of the old terminology and traditions, but they've changed their mission. Cupcake Cadets International is a global corporation that is creating go-getters, career women, women who won't take no for an answer. Today, Cadets are prepared to succeed. No, to excel."

"Yeah," Slater said. "We're discovering that."

"What's important is to *discover* a way out of this," Ruthie said. "As far as I know, Margaret Parsley doesn't have any older brothers or sisters I can talk to."

"She's an only child," Slater said. "I saw it on the family tree she made for her Genealogy Caliber Badge."

"Then I've got no sway over her," Ruthie said. "And she's got that photo of you so you're stuck following through with the Windjammer Whirl."

"But we can't," Jeremy said. "We don't have enough badges to qualify."

"Not to mention cupcake sales," Slater said. "After Margaret dumped her leftovers on us, we're back to square one."

"Square zero," Jeremy muttered.

"It looks like you girls are stuck," Ruthie spun in her chair and got up. "Have fun at the Windjammer Whirl!"

"This is never going to work," Slater said as they made their way to the Elks Lodge the next day in full Cupcake Cadet uniform.

Jeremy hoisted the buckets onto his shoulder and tugged the red wagon behind him. "Of course it's going to work. You gave me the idea."

"I did?"

"Sure," Jeremy said. "Remember when we were at the firehouse?"

"The day I slid down the pole?"

"That's the day."

Slater grinned as he thought about it. "That was awesome."

"You offered a service with the purchase of a cupcake. You told the firefighters if they bought twenty cupcakes we would polish their fire truck for free." Jeremy tugged the wagon over the edge of the curb. "That was a good idea, but if people don't want the product you're selling, the service becomes less important."

"I've lost you."

"I want to flip it around," Jeremy said. "Offer a service and throw in free cupcakes. The guys at the Elks Lodge agreed we could use their parking lot and their hoses. I've got the buckets, the sponges, and the soap. . . ."

Jeremy reached into the wagon and pulled out a poster board. He taped it to the flagpole and stepped back to inspect his handiwork. The sign read:

This weekend only!!

CUPCAKE CADETS CAR WASH
Exterior cleaning of your vehicle: Only $8

FREE WITH CAR WASH:
Your choice of delicious cupcakes

(while supplies last)

"I've got it all figured out," Jeremy said. "We have to do nineteen cars each to earn the money we'll need to enter the tournament. That's a breeze! Just soap it up, rinse it off, and bam! Eight bucks in our hands."

Slater thought about the plan. "Are there nineteen dirty cars in town?"

"There had better be," Jeremy said. "Actually, there had better be thirty-eight."

The morning started slowly. Jeremy and Slater sat on the low wall by the street watching the cars roll by. As it turned out, there were plenty of dirty cars, but no one seemed to want to turn in to the Elks Club parking lot. A few people paused to read the sign, but no one stopped. Although Jeremy had brought along lunch, he was giving thought to calling it quits at noon and heading home.

"What are you two up to?" It was Angelina. Her voice sounded cold. She was headed up the block, a loaded wagon behind her.

"What's it look like?" Slater said.

Jeremy jumped in. "She means to say we're holding a car wash."

Angelina looked at the empty buckets and piles of dry rags. "Having much luck with that?"

Neither Jeremy nor Slater answered.

"Yeah, that's what my mother told me," Angelina said.

"Your mother?" Slater asked.

"She drove by before. Called to tell me you were struggling out here." Angelina bumped her sneaker against her wagon. "Have you ever even *held* a car wash before?" she asked.

Jeremy shrugged. "We've washed our dad's car before."

"We know how to do it, if that's what you're getting at," Slater said. "It's not like you can screw up soapy water."

Angelina tucked her blond hair behind one ear. "Samantha, I'm not trying to rub anything in, but there are right ways and wrong ways to do a car wash." She walked to the sign and tugged it off the flagpole.

"Hey, what are you—" Jeremy began, but Angelina stopped him with a stern glance.

"Watch and learn."

She walked to the side of the street, held the sign over her head, and began to wave it around. She smiled and started stepping from side to side like she was doing some sort of dance. "My mom has had me in ballet since I was five, but I really love hip-hop."

Angelina told Jeremy and Slater the names of the

different steps as she did them. "This is the Glide . . . this is the Harlem Shuffle . . . this is the Heel-Toe . . . and this one is the SpongeBob."

After a few seconds of the SpongeBob, Jeremy began to get dizzy. "How did you learn all this stuff?" he asked.

"YouTube, of course. Now, let me do my thing and you do yours . . . washing cars."

Within moments, the first car pulled up. It was Ms. Jakob with her nephew Karl. She was driving her new convertible. "Exterior wash, huh?" she said.

"*And* a free cupcake?" Karl said excitedly. He turned to his aunt. "Can we get a car wash? *Pleeeeease?*"

Ms. Jakob nodded and pulled out her purse. "Go to work, ladies."

Jeremy and Slater leaped up and started hosing down the car while Angelina did her dance moves and waved the sign around. After several more cars drove up, she pulled out her cell phone.

"Who are you calling?" Jeremy asked her.

"You don't think two girls with sponges is enough, do you? Ever heard of reinforcements?"

Before long, the parking lot was filled with Cadets.

"Hey!" Angelina called over to Slater. "We're going to need another sign waver. How are your moves?"

Slater perked up. "I just finished level twelve of Dance Floor Disco Breaker!" he cried out.

Angelina grinned. "Well, show me your Beverly Hills Boogaloo!"

Slater darted to the sidewalk and began strutting back and forth in front of a row of mailboxes. His dance moves weren't nearly as expert as Angelina's, but they were certainly as entertaining. He shook his tail and kicked his legs like he was a giant chicken trying to scratch at the ground.

"Ha!" Angelina said. "But can you do this?" She spun halfway around and started kicking her heels to her backside one after the other.

"The Seattle Stomp?" Slater said dismissively. "That's level four. Try this!"

Slater and Angelina kept challenging each other to different moves. Before long, Slater had his skateboard out and the two of them were dancing, gliding up and down the sidewalk, and grinding along the curbs. Slater matched every one of Angelina's dance moves and she matched every one of his skateboard tricks. All the while, they kept pumping their signs in the air.

"Where'd you learn to board like that?" he asked her.

"My cousin taught me last summer. Guess my ballet

training came to some good, huh?"

The rest of the girls soaped, rinsed, and dried. A few of the girls brought hand vacuums and window cleaner and added an upcharge for interior cleaning (along with an extra free cupcake). One girl brought a tire buffer. Another brought her portable stereo so they could play music while they worked (and so Angelina and Slater would have something to dance to). And all of them brought their cupcakes. Wagons, boxes, handcarts, and backpacks filled with them. Before long, the poster looked like this:

This weekend only!!
CUPCAKE CADETS CAR WASH
Exterior cleaning of your vehicle: Only $8
FREE WITH CAR WASH:
Your choice of delicious cupcakes
(while supplies last)
Interior vacuum and windows: Add $4
Supershine wheels: Add $2
THE WORKS!!!! $15

As he was soaping up Mr. Madison's SUV (vans and trucks were twelve dollars) Jeremy called over to

Angelina. "I thought most of you already sold your cupcakes."

She laughed. "Are you kidding? We got scooped by the Thomas Scolari Academy for Boys. They started their popcorn sale a full week before our shipment came in. Cupcake sales have been flatter than flat."

Jeremy had heard about that. Every year, the soccer team held a popcorn sale to help fund their trip to the state soccer tournament. According to Coach Jenkins, it was Paul Vogler's idea to start selling early in order to beat the Cupcake Cadets to the punch. With the rest of town stuffed past capacity with Caramel Cocoa Crunch and Adirondack Moose Track popcorn (along with six other delicious gourmet varieties), no one was interested in vacuum-packaged cupcakes with a two-year shelf life.

"When we heard you guys were doing the car wash, and how you came up with a way to unload cupcakes, we had to get in on it." She kicked her leg to the side and spun around. "This idea is totally genius!"

By evening, the parking lot was filled with heaps of wet rags, stacks of empty buckets, and piles of exhausted Cupcake Cadets. The girls were sprawled wherever they dropped, on the lawn, the sidewalk, or the low stone wall in front of the Elks Lodge. What the parking lot was *not* filled with was cupcakes. Virtually all the cupcakes were gone and Jeremy's pockets were filled with cash.

A blue van pulled up and a horn tooted.

Jeremy's stomach flip-flopped.

His father's van. "Got time for one more?" his dad called out the driver's window.

The girls groaned.

"The youngest Cadets have to wash that one," Slater said, turning away so Mr. Bender would not recognize him.

"Actually, it goes by seniority," Cheryl Cahill said. She was propped against a mailbox, her sore arms hanging to either side. "You and Jenna are the newest Cadets, so get cleaning."

Angelina nodded in agreement. "She's right."

"Bylaw 2042-A, Section Three," Cheryl added.

"Yeah, page ninety-four of the manual," Jeremy said. "I know. But this car wash was our idea. If we hadn't thought of it . . ."

Cheryl snapped her fingers and pointed at the van. "Get washing."

Soaked, exhausted, and now terrified, Jeremy combed his fingers through his fake hair so it covered as much of his face as possible. Why couldn't Ruthie have bought a longer wig?

Jeremy and Slater began at the back of the van and worked the sponges as slowly as possible. As they moved closer to the front of the vehicle, the passenger window rolled down. Ruthie peered out, an evil grin across her face. "Come on, girls. We don't have all day."

Jeremy heard his father. "Ruth, be nice. It wasn't so long ago that you were a Cadet."

The window rolled back up and the boys continued. They washed both sides, then crawled around to the front bumper and grille.

"Are you ready to do this?" Jeremy asked Slater from below the level of the hood.

Slater shook his head. "What choice do we have?"

Jeremy gave his hair one final adjustment, held his breath, and stood.

Slater stood next to him and the two started washing the hood of the van.

Jeremy heard Ruthie's laughter through the windshield. He peered at his sister, who was staring at him and smiling. Jeremy kept his head down and worked the sponge as quickly as he could. Finally, when he was making his way down the driver's side, Jeremy peeked at his father. He was fiddling with the knobs on the stereo. Ruthie, on the other hand, still had her eyes glued to Jeremy as though seeing him in a Cupcake Cadet uniform was the most satisfying form of entertainment the world had ever known.

When the boys finished, Ruthie rolled down her window. She handed him twelve dollars.

"What, no tip?"

"You really want a tip?" Ruthie asked him.

"Of course I do."

She looked him up and down. "Your Apricot Sprinkle lip gloss clashes with your sash."

Then she rolled up her window and their father drove away.

Burnt or Baked?

At the very next meeting of the Cupcake Cadets, the girls sat quietly as Ms. Rendell stared across the circle at Jeremy and Slater.

"I just don't know what to make of you," she said.

"What's to make?" Jeremy asked.

"For the past few months you two have been absolute terrors. Now, here in the eleventh hour, you come through with a cupcake sale to end all cupcake sales."

"And it wasn't even a cupcake sale," Slater added, grinning. "It was a car wash!"

"That part is clear to me," Ms. Rendell said. "I

was ready to break the news to you today, to tell you your chances of racing in the Windjammer Whirl were over. . . ." She drifted off.

"But . . ." Slater said. He dug his pinkie into a hole he had worn through his purple-and-pink-striped tights.

Ms. Rendell pursed her lips. "I've given this a great deal of thought, and—"

"Ms. Rendell, you can't," Margaret cut in. "You've got to earn badges one at a time."

"Says who?" said Angelina.

"She's trying to invoke Rule 1324-B, Section One-A," Jeremy said. A few of the younger girls in the circle opened their handbooks and started flipping through the pages.

"It's the single-badge rule," Margaret said to the girls.

"What about Rule 9432-B, Section Nine?" Angelina protested.

The girls began flipping pages in the opposite direction.

Jeremy sighed. "It is the rule that says the troop leader has the right to make exceptions to the rules."

"Jenna and Samantha had a great idea and it helped everyone," Angelina said. "We all needed the cupcake sales. You're just mad that you didn't think of it first."

"I don't know a thing about all these rules." Slater pulled out an envelope and opened it to reveal a stack of bills. "What I *do* know is that we unloaded a ton of cupcakes." He tossed the money to Ms. Rendell. "You've all sold your quotas."

A happy-sounding buzz spread through the auditorium. Ms. Rendell began counting the money while the girls began whispering among themselves.

Slater tapped Jeremy on the shoulder. "I still don't know why we're doing this," he whispered. "This would have given us the perfect excuse not to compete. We would have been in the clear, dude."

Jeremy looked over Slater's shoulder. Margaret was staring at him, eyes narrowed to slits. "Because of her," he said. "This is bigger than fixing my father's engine. This is bigger than boys versus the Cupcake Cadets. This is about winning. It's about us beating Margaret Parsley and her evil, pinched-up face."

Ms. Rendell called the room to attention with a few claps of her hands. "I've made up my mind about Jenna and Samantha," she said. She smiled at the boys.

"Noooo!" Margaret cried out.

* * *

Jeremy gazed at himself in the full-length mirror that leaned against the wall of the icehouse. He smoothed down his wig. The three badges he had sewn on his uniform seemed to gleam, to dance.

After the short debate at the cadet meeting earlier that day, Ms. Rendell made the announcement. Since Jenna and Samantha had sold well beyond their quota of cupcakes, she exercised her right to bend the rules as provided by Rule 9432-B Section Nine and awarded Jenna and Samantha the three badges they needed.

The boys could compete in the Windjammer Whirl.

The first badge was bright green with a dollar sign on it. Below the emblem it read: *SALES SUPERSTAR.* Ms. Rendell gave it to them for conceiving of and executing the car wash (and for bringing in so much money to the Cupcake Cadets).

Their next badge was blue. It had a silver cash register with a wide grin on it. Beneath the picture it read: *SERVICE WITH A SMILE.* Ms. Rendell awarded the badge for their excellent service. According to what she heard from her daughter, Bailey, they ran a quick and efficient car wash and handled all complaints—every accidental streak and every drip mark—with professionalism and courtesy.

The third badge was red with a crossed wrench and screwdriver on it. At the bottom it read: *AUTO REPAIR*. Word got to Ms. Rendell that Jeremy had suggested the girls perform minor vehicle repairs and maintenance for customers, too. Simple things like replacing ratty wiper blades and checking oil and windshield fluid levels, all stuff that he could do blindfolded (as long as there was no grape or orange soda around). He had two of the girls making runs to Arty's Auto Parts and was upcharging between three and ten dollars depending on labor.

A bunch of the others earned badges, too. Things like Marketing Wiz, Financial Fiend, and two Dancing Frenzy badges (those went to Angelina and Slater for their marathon moves that brought in the cars in droves).

The gilded thread woven into the badges caused them to glimmer in the light. He thought back to the first time he had put on the Cupcake Cadet uniform, when he was cowering behind the boat. These days he wore his uniform fearlessly.

The secret knock sounded on the door and Jeremy opened it. Slater stood there, his backpack slung over one shoulder.

"Had to stop home for some model glue and a can of spray paint." He pushed into the icehouse and looked Jeremy over. "Why are you still wearing your uniform? The meeting ended a half hour ago."

"I don't know," Jeremy said. "I just haven't had a chance to take it off yet."

All Slater could say was, "Dude . . ."

Cookies, Tea, and Larceny

"This is so boring," Slater whispered to Jeremy. "They've been talking for a half hour and there's no end in sight."

"Be quiet and drink your tea," Jeremy said. "I see victory on the horizon."

Slater slouched in his seat. "I see a storm cloud," he muttered.

The tables were arranged around four blue kiddie pools. Jeremy could make out different obstacles floating in the water: an arch made of drinking straws, a sponge slalom course, and several rubber duckies.

The boys sat toward the back and were the only

ones without their parents present. The rest of the girls sat clustered with their respective troops in different corners of the auditorium. Troop 224, the girls who beat them at field hockey, looked bigger than ever and met Jeremy's glances with bloodthirsty glares.

Ms. Rendell was standing behind a podium and spoke into a microphone alongside the other troop leaders. "I can't begin to describe the amount of dedication the Cadets of Troop One Forty-Nine have shown to make sure this year's Windjammer Whirl is a success."

Mrs. Sanchez leaned toward the microphone and said, "Troop Two Twenty-four has had a record year as well. I just wanted to acknowledge them."

Ms. Rendell rolled her eyes and readjusted the mike so it was farther from Mrs. Sanchez's lipsticked mouth. "And remember," Ms. Rendell went on. "This is a friendly competition. We hope the Windjammer Whirl helps to foster a sense of hard work and friendly competition."

This time, it was Mrs. Sanchez who rolled her eyes. She leaned across the podium. "And our judges will be on the lookout, girls." She looked pointedly at Ms. Rendell. "There is reason to believe that there have been some shenanigans these past few years that have altered the outcome of the event."

Ms. Rendell looked aghast. Jeremy scanned the room for Margaret. She was frozen, holding a tray of cookies near the food table. She looked furious.

If Jeremy didn't know the Cupcake Cadet motto— that whole caring, cooperation, and a little vanilla frosting thing—he would have thought Ms. Rendell and Mrs. Sanchez were about to pounce on each other and start pulling hair. He would have thought the whole room was about to break out into a no-holds-barred brawl.

Slater nudged Jeremy. "Um, have you noticed our boat isn't very girly?" he whispered.

Looking around the auditorium, Jeremy noticed that most of the other boats were pink or purple and flowery. If there was an opposite of pink, purple, and flowery, their boat was it. The boys had glued the cracked mast and repainted the hull with silver spray paint. Jeremy had written the words *SILVER BULLET* in large block letters down the side and had scribbled a few lightning bolts and a skull and crossbones with a Sharpie marker.

"Who's to say this isn't girly?" Jeremy asked, picking up the windjammer. "What makes lightning bolts and skulls a boy thing?"

"Because they're cool?" Slater dug his fingernails into his thighs and ran them up and down. "These new tights are so itchy. Who would invent itchy tights?"

"Probably some man." It was Margaret. She walked up with Angelina, who was holding a cup of punch. Margaret clutched a spiral notebook to her chest and kept peering around to inspect other windjammers around the auditorium.

"How are you enjoying the tea social?" Angelina asked.

"Pretty cool," Jeremy said.

"Don't do anything to screw it up," Margaret warned.

"Don't be rude," Angelina said to her.

"After what they've put us through this year, I could be ruder," Margaret muttered.

"I see you have some tea," Angelina said, clearly hoping to change the subject. "How about some cookies? They are over on the food table."

Before either of them could answer, Margaret said, "Aren't you worried they might drown in the punch bowl?"

"Hey—" Slater began.

"Interesting paint job," Angelina said. "Is it supposed to be a pirate ship? I love pirates."

"Something like that," Jeremy said.

"It was my idea," Slater boasted. "I figured every boat would be pink and purple and that flowers would be overdone."

"Oh." Angelina sounded hurt. "Mine is, uh, pink and purple with a flower on the sail."

"I didn't mean . . ."

Angelina smiled. "I'm just kidding. Mine's only pink, no purple."

"Not a bad design," Margaret said, inspecting the boys' boat. "I like how you tapered the stern. Have you tested her out yet?"

Jeremy shook his head. "Today is her maiden voyage."

"Technique matters," Margaret said as she started to walk off. "You two are going to be soggy toast."

"Don't count on it," Jeremy said. "We're not going down without a fight."

"Yes, you are," Margaret said. "My new design is going to blow that thing out of the water."

"Oh yeah?" Slater said. "What's it look like?"

"Wouldn't you like to know? My boat is wrapped

with a cloth diaper, sealed in a Ziploc bag, and snapped tight in a Tupperware container so it won't absorb unnecessary moisture. It's under lock and key. Super secret." She pointed to her table, where the container sat alone. She shook her head. "Where did my parents go?" she said. "They were supposed to sit there and guard my windjammer!"

"They're getting some tea," Angelina said, pointing to the snack table.

Margaret dashed off but Angelina lingered behind. "Your lip gloss is smudged," she said to Slater.

His fingers went to his mouth. "Oh, probably from the cookies or the teacup or something," he said. "No biggie."

Angelina scoffed. "Of course it's a biggie," she said. "Today is the Windjammer Whirl." She opened her purse, pulled out a small tube, and handed it to Slater. "It's Cherry Lime Pie."

"Uh, thanks," Slater said. He began to put it in his pocket.

"No, use it now. I need it back."

Slater looked at Jeremy, then back to Angelina.

"Go on," she said. "It's not like I have cooties or anything."

Slater hesitantly uncapped the tube and ran it over his mouth. He pressed his lips together to smooth everything out and handed the tube back.

"Much better," Angelina said. "Now, I ought to find Margaret before she melts down. Good luck later on!"

When Angelina was beyond earshot, Jeremy said, "Dude."

"Shut up."

"But, dude."

"Shut . . . up . . ."

"Dude!"

"I said shut up!"

Jeremy shut up.

After a few more minutes of mixing and mingling, of tea drinking and cookie nibbling, Ms. Rendell approached the podium and tapped the microphone. "I'd like to ask everyone to have a seat now." The microphone gave a squeak and she pulled her mouth away from it. "Please settle down, people."

Ms. Rendell thanked the other troops for attending, the regional director (lovingly called the Big Muffin) for her dedication, and the good people from the home office in Missoula, Montana, for coming up with the idea of the Windjammer Whirl in the first place. Then, everyone recited the Pledge of Allegiance and sang the official Cupcake Cadet Song, "Everything Tastes Better With Frosting":

"I'll use teamwork and cooperation,

and innovative thinking.

I'll use caring and sharing,

and a bit of vanilla frosting. . . ."

Jeremy's fingers played over his Caliber Badges as he sang along. All the while, his mind raced. What he and Slater were doing had nothing to do with teamwork and cooperation, or with caring and sharing. It sure as heck had nothing to do with vanilla frosting. A heavy feeling weighed down his gut. Jeremy figured this was what guilt must feel like.

He had to confess. It was the right thing to do. He had to withdraw from the Windjammer Whirl.

Jeremy's hand moved to the shiny blond wig he had been hiding behind for so long. After months of wearing it, the fake hair felt like part of him. He balled up his fist, ready to yank the wig from his head. He stood and cleared his throat.

Just then, a scream pierced the air from the far corner of the auditorium. Everyone spun to see where it came from. It was Margaret. She was standing, shaking. Her chair flopped backward behind her. The Tupperware container that supposedly held her windjammer shook in her hands. She cried out: "Who . . . took . . . my . . . boat?"

The Cupcake Inquisition

Margaret's fiery gaze scanned the auditorium as though every attendee were a suspect. When her eyes landed on Jeremy, they narrowed to the evil slits he was getting so used to seeing. He left the wig in place and let his hand drop to his lap. This was not the time to admit any sort of wrongdoing. He and Slater already had a bad enough reputation with Ms. Rendell and the troop.

He sat down as Margaret pointed a finger at him.

Just then, Cheryl Cahill came running from the bathroom. She held a mass of broken wood with a busted mast and crushed sail, what used to be a shiny blue windjammer. The model boat was flat, as though someone had stomped on it with a military boot. "Margaret! Margaret!" she cried. "Your boat! Someone smashed your boat!"

Margaret grabbed what was left of her boat and fled the auditorium. Her parents chased after her. The rest of the girls from Troop 149 turned their accusatory stares to Jeremy and Slater. Everyone, that is, except Angelina. She looked at them with an expression of sadness, pity maybe.

"Please," Mrs. Sanchez said from the podium. "Please, everyone take a seat." When the noise reduced to a low rumble, she went on. "It saddens me that the ideals we talk about at every meeting and at every event could be forgotten so easily because of a trophy or a cash prize. Everyone knows Margaret Parsley has been the winner for several years now and I know my girls in particular were looking forward to competing with her. Let's take a short break so we can figure out what to do. We'll be racing those windjammers before you know it." She snapped her fingers at her Cadets. "Girls, please refill everyone's tea and bring around some more cookies."

"How could you do such a thing?" It was Angelina.

Behind her stood a few of the other girls from the troop.

"We didn't—"

"What do you expect us to think?" she said. "Everything that's gone wrong this year, it's because of you."

"We were sitting here the whole time!" Slater said. "You were talking with us. The pink-and-purple boat with flowers. The lip gloss. Remember?"

"Come on," she said. "You knew Margaret's boat would win. We all knew it. She wins every year. That's no reason to sabotage her project."

"Margaret works ten times as hard as all of us put together," some other girl added. "It's all she lives for."

"At least she should be able to compete," Angelina said.

"We didn't do anything," Jeremy said, his voice suddenly sounding very boyish.

Angelina crossed her arms over her chest. "We'll see about that."

After the girls stalked off and the boys had a chance to breathe again, Slater said, "So, who do you think did it?"

Jeremy shook his head. "No idea. Margaret might be a pain, but that was totally mean."

"*Totally mean* is right." It was Margaret. Her voice was calm and level, almost creepily calm and level considering how red her face was.

"Look, Margaret—"

She held up a hand to silence Jeremy. "I'm not sure who destroyed my boat, but I'm pretty sure it wasn't you guys. You might be inconsiderate and you might not respect what we Cadets do, but you're not stupid."

"So what are you going to do?" Slater asked. "There's no way you can race that boat."

Margaret dropped her mangled windjammer on the table and settled into a seat across from them. She leaned in close. "Considering the favor I'm doing for you by not mentioning your secret to Ms. Rendell . . ." Margaret reached across the table and slid the boys' boat toward herself. She lowered her head and eyeballed down the length of it. "*Your* boat is now officially *my* boat."

"No way!" Slater cried out.

"Way," Margaret said. "As of this moment, I'm on Team Jenna and Samantha. I already spoke to Ms. Rendell about it. I told her that I helped you with your design and asked if it would be all right if I led your team to victory." Margaret leaned back in her chair.

"Of course, she agreed."

Jeremy wanted to argue with her, but what was the point? If they won, she was getting half the prize money anyway. What was the difference if she was on their team or not? Besides, Jeremy felt bad for Margaret. Anyone who worked so hard on her boat deserved to be in the competition.

Margaret stood. "Ms. Rendell said we could use the conference room to prepare. We've got thirty minutes. Let's get moving."

Slater laid out both boats on the conference table: Ruthie's design and what was left of Margaret's. Margaret laid out the tools she had brought: scissors, a clamp, a file, a pair of pliers, and a bottle of quick-drying glue. But what could they do in such a short time?

Jeremy examined Margaret's windjammer. It was a lump of broken wood, squashed beyond anything that might be called a boat, but Jeremy could imagine what it had looked like before being destroyed. He could see how putting outriggers on the hull would lend more stability. He saw how she had carefully flattened the bottom to allow it to turn more easily. And he hadn't even thought of putting multiple sails on two masts to allow for better steering.

Margaret picked up the boys' silver boat and examined it more closely. "It's not terrible, but we'll have to make some modifications. Grab some Quickie Glue and do what I say."

"Good thing your sister was so good at this," Slater said to Jeremy.

Margaret's eyes narrowed. "Your sister?" she asked.

Jeremy nodded. "My sister was a Cadet a few years ago. This is her boat. All we did was repaint it."

Margaret pounded her fist on the table so hard that both windjammers hopped into the air. "You guys are such screwups. I knew I recognized this boat from somewhere. This is Ruthie Bender's boat, isn't it? It was my first year in the Cadets. She won second place behind Lisa Payne. It's the boat that inspired me."

"At least my dearest sis has inspired someone," Jeremy said.

"This isn't a joke. I can't use someone else's design. That is outright cheating, not to mention a violation of Bylaw 2041-A Section Three." Margaret clenched her jaw and turned her watery eyes to the ceiling. "Ugh. I am so not going to cry in front of you. I told Ms. Rendell that I helped you design this boat. If we don't use it, I'm the one lying!"

"Sorry," Jeremy said.

"Not as sorry as I am." Margaret sighed. "But one thing is for sure."

"What's that?" Jeremy asked.

"The only way to stick it to whoever smashed my boat is to win the Windjammer Whirl."

Slater reached into his official Cupcake Cadet shoulder satchel and pulled out a brand-new model windjammer box. He dumped the contents on the table: an unfinished block of wood, a dowel for the mast, and a piece of plastic for the sail.

"I can't believe I'm even suggesting this," Slater said, "but let's get started."

Ready, Set, Blow!

When they came out of the conference room, the auditorium was abuzz. Instead of holding a modified silver boat or a rebuilt blue boat, Jeremy, Slater, and Margaret came out with something new, something different, and something that looked as though it would sink like a stone. The hull was the unpainted block with the edges filed down. The front tapered as best they could make it taper with only a file and ten minutes. Blue, taped-up outriggers from Margaret's original design stretched from either side, and the silver mast from Ruthie's boat rose from the deck. Multiple sails sprung from the mast like roses on a rod-straight vine. They had coated it with a quick layer of clear nail polish, and Slater had written the name SS *MEGAWEDGIE* down the side with a Sharpie marker.

"SS *MEGAWEDGIE*?" Jeremy asked.

Slater shrugged. "It sort of looks like a wedge, doesn't it?"

"No," Margaret said. "It looks like a brick."

According to the elimination brackets, they were in the first heat, so Margaret knelt beside the pool. The auditorium went silent. "Sink or swim time," she said as she lowered their boat into the water.

The windjammer bobbed for a few seconds, then settled. It seemed to struggle to stay afloat, but fortunately for them it was swim time.

The room came alive with cheering. The extra weight of their hull was sure to slow them down, but Jeremy hoped what they lacked in speed they would make up for in design innovation. After all, innovative thinking was one of the things Cupcake Cadets was all about.

"Watch how I keep my head low to keep the boat from tipping over," she told them. "Keep an eye on how fast I move around the pool. Lots of tiny breaths are better than one big gust, but once you're on the final straightaway, it's every girl for herself. Oh, and don't bump into the pool. It'll send a wave across the water that'll knock your boat off course."

Jeremy gave her a thumbs-up. "Go ahead and win it," he said.

Slater stuffed a cookie in his mouth and Margaret glared at him.

"What?" he said. "I get hungry when I'm nervous."

There were four troops participating, one for each kiddie pool, and a boat only moved on to the next round when it had won three races. Jeremy knew it wasn't going to be easy, but for once he agreed with Margaret. The only way to stick it to whoever smashed Margaret's boat was to win the Windjammer Whirl.

The head referee lifted both arms and called for quiet. After running through the basic rules and complimenting Margaret's team for quick thinking and cooperation, she called out, "Ready! Set! Blow!" Then she tweeted her whistle.

Huff and Puff and
Blow Your Boat In!

The Windjammer Whirl was much harder than Jeremy had imagined. These girls were fierce! They scrambled around the kiddie pools like crazed chimps. They blew through the straws as though they were doing delicate surgery. Yet, they cheered each other on—loud and long—as though there wasn't a five-hundred-dollar prize for the winner.

"Nothing like the calm girl from the library poster." Slater stuffed another cookie in his mouth. "You said this was going to be a cakewalk."

"I said it would be a *cupcake* walk," Jeremy said. "And it looks like I was wrong."

But Margaret deserved her reputation as the best. Sure, she might have done loads of research and had an excellent design, but her expertise did not stop there. She sent that boat around the course like a pro. She scampered around like the most agile of chimps, was more precise with her straw than any surgeon, and did not touch the edge of the kiddie pool once. The least Jeremy and Slater could do was cheer her on.

And they were loud.

It was no surprise who came in first. Margaret crossed the finish line a mile ahead of the next closest team. The judge placed a small X next to their boat's name on the leader board to denote the win.

It was time for round two and Slater volunteered. As he approached the pool, he pulled two straws from his pocket.

"Excuse me," Margaret said. "What are you doing?"

"It's my patented two-straw technique," he said. "I use one to blow the sails and the other to blow the back of the boat when I need to turn. It's just like skateboarding."

Jeremy laughed. "There's no rule prohibiting it," he said. "The rulebook states—"

"Don't quote the rulebook at me," Margaret said. "It's just that we have a lot riding on this."

Slater held up a hand and smiled. "Have faith."

"That's easier said than done." Margaret bumped Slater on the shoulder with her fist. "You'd better not screw this up."

And Slater did not screw anything up. Using what he called "kick turns," Slater maneuvered their windjammer through the obstacle course—under every arch, through every tunnel, and around every rubber ducky—faster than anyone thought a windjammer could move. Although he bumped the pool twice with his knee, Slater still won in the end.

As the judges marked their second X on the leader board, Jeremy squatted beside the pool. "Guess I'm next," he said.

Slater held out his extra straw. "Want to try my technique?"

Jeremy shook his head. "Wouldn't want to have to borrow your girlfriend's lip gloss," he said. "Anyhow, I've never been much of a boarder. I'm going to win this with sheer lung power."

"You sure?" he said.

"You know how much I like to talk," Jeremy said. "My lungs are in world-class shape."

Slater grinned. "Go for it, dude." They bumped knuckles.

Jeremy looked up to see Margaret standing over him. She held out a fist too. "Go for it, dude," she said.

Jeremy bumped knuckles with her, then hunched over the kiddie pool ready for the starting whistle.

TWEET!!!

Jeremy puffed their windjammer down the first stretch and scampered around the pool to make the first turn. Keeping that boat on course was harder than he had imagined. It was as if the boat had a mind of its own and it wanted to be anywhere but where Jeremy needed it to go. Nevertheless, he managed to navigate the obstacles with reasonable ease. The twin masts were working great and he did not bump the pool. It's true he nearly passed out in the home stretch from puffing too hard, but the SS *MEGAWEDGIE* glided across the finish line with a huge cheer from Troop 149. Ms. Rendell beamed.

Margaret clapped Jeremy and Slater on the backs. "Round two, ladies," she said. "This competition is about to heat up."

A Dizzying Finish

Whether as a result of Margaret's scrappiness, Jeremy's lung power, or Slater's kick turns, heat after heat Jeremy's team came out on top. As their competitors thinned, the races became tighter and tighter, but each round Team SS *MEGAWEDGIE* glided across the finish line with three Xs next to its name.

In the final round, it was Jeremy blowing against Sophie, the girl from the field hockey game with shoulders wider than a linebacker's. *Her lungs,* Jeremy thought, *must be bigger than bagpipes.*

The Corinth boat was painted glossy black with neon pink pinstripes that curved along the sleek hull. Pink lettering down the sides read *CUPCAKE CARNAGE,* and the girls had painted bloody shark teeth on the front. The boat rode low in the water with a sail that seemed to capture the air and use every bit of it to rocket forward.

Each team had won exactly two races, so the winner of this last heat decided the champion of this year's Windjammer Whirl.

"Good luck," Jeremy said to Sophie. Against every urge, he extended his hand to shake.

"Like I'm going to need it," she spat back.

Margaret tugged Jeremy away before he could say anything in return. "Don't worry about her," she said.

"I'm not worrying," Jeremy said. "I'm just wondering if that's really a 'her.'"

"You would know better than anyone," Margaret said, smiling. It might be the first smile Jeremy had ever seen on Margaret and it suited her. "We can win this thing," she went on. "We just have to want it more."

Jeremy kneeled beside the pool and lifted the straw to his lips. He bent over the water and took a few deep breaths. Looking to his right, he surveyed his competition. Sophie scowled at him as she hunched over the boat bobbing in front of her.

The judge gave a single tweet of her whistle and explained the situation: "Here we are, ladies, in the final heat. We are down to two teams, one from Corinth and one from Snydersville. Both teams have two Xs on the board, meaning the next boat to cross the finish line wins this year's Windjammer Whirl. I want this to be a clean race and I want you all to think about what it means to be a Cupcake Cadet . . ." The judge paused before she went on. "Are there any questions?"

No one said a word.

"All right, then. Team SS *MEGAWEDGIE*, are you ready?"

Jeremy lifted his straw to his lips and nodded.

"Team *CUPCAKE CARNAGE*, are you ready?"

Sophie nodded.

"At the sound of my whistle the race begins."

She raised the silver whistle to her lips and . . .

TWEEEEEEEEET!!!

Jeremy puffed through his straw. Due to a misaim, the SS *MEGAWEDGIE* got a sluggish start, but Jeremy corrected and the boat glided down the straightaway and through the first floating arch. He took a deep breath and scrambled to the left, urging his boat into the first turn. The cheers were almost deafening and he could hear dozens of people chanting his name.

"Jen-na! Jen-na! Jen-na!"

Jeremy puffed their windjammer under the second bendy straw arch and through a long tunnel. He glanced up to see Paul standing next to Ms. Rendell. He wore a huge smile across his face and was cheering louder than anyone.

Jeremy puffed at the boat some more until he reached what he thought was the hardest part of the challenge, the slalom. However, his technique had improved over the course of the day. Scampering from left to right with little puffs on the side sails worked best and Jeremy realized Margaret's mast design was working really well.

Three times around the rubber ducky was the last obstacle and Jeremy circled it like a master. It was like he was willing that boat through the course with his mind rather than with his lungs. Sophie was having trouble getting her boat around the ducky so Jeremy had the advantage, but that advantage was at risk. His windjammer was all about maneuverability, but *CUPCAKE CARNAGE* was the faster boat, and the final leg of the race was a straightaway.

Jeremy sucked in a deep breath to really get

his windjammer moving. That's when the dizziness overcame him like someone had slipped a black bag over his head. The last thoughts that crossed Jeremy's mind as he fainted were (in no particular order):

That water sure is rushing up at me fast.

Boy, I could really go for a slice of Mom's caramel apple walnut pie.

I hope my wig doesn't come off when I pass ou . . .

Wigless in Snydersville

By the time Jeremy regained consciousness, his head in Ms. Rendell's lap, the Windjammer Whirl had turned to utter chaos. His hand immediately went to his head and he felt only his real hair. Jeremy looked at Slater, who had been de-tammed as well. Team *CUPCAKE CARNAGE* and the rest of the Corinth Cadets were stomping around the auditorium chanting, "We rule! We rule! We rule!" over and over. Parents were complaining to the officials and the Cadets were complaining to one another about how there should be a rematch. The fact that boys had infiltrated the race meant the competition should start over again. Mrs.

Sanchez, of course, was arguing otherwise and leading her girls to the podium to receive their trophy and the five-hundred-dollar oversized novelty check.

Jeremy struggled to sit up, but Ms. Rendell held him down with a gentle touch. "Stay put," she said, disappointment in her voice. "Let them blow off steam for a while."

"I'm fine." Jeremy sat up, still woozy. Facing his father over the damaged boat seemed like nothing compared to the havoc he had wreaked by joining the Cupcake Cadets.

TWEEEEEET!

The judge blew her whistle and everyone fell silent. Jeremy hoisted his soaking wet Cupcake-Cadet-uniform-wearing body into a nearby chair.

Ms. Rendell stepped to the microphone. "Everyone," she said. "If you wouldn't mind waiting a moment while we sort everything out."

"What's to sort out?" Mrs. Sanchez hollered. "I can understand getting a little help here and there, but bringing in boys to win the Windjammer Whirl?"

Jeremy wanted to go up there, to explain every-thing, but he knew better than to stand between two charging bulls.

"I need to discuss this matter with the girls."

"What girls?" Mrs. Sanchez said. "How low can you sink?"

"How low can *I* sink?" Ms. Rendell said.

That's when Jeremy stood up. Charging bulls or not, he made his way to the podium. His sneakers squeaked with each step as he weaved between the tables, between the kiddie pools, and up onto the low riser. Water dripped down his forehead and plastered his hair to his skull. Jeremy looked out at the crowd. There had to be a hundred people. Their expressions ranged from confusion to betrayal to outright anger.

Jeremy angled the microphone to his face and opened his mouth to talk. He had to say something. He'd seen this sort of thing on television a thousand times. The kid who screwed up comes clean. He announces that he screwed up, but that he'd learned a valuable lesson. Then he tells everyone what he learned—maybe sheds a tear or two—and everyone applauds.

He looked up at Ms. Rendell, whose head was wagging side to side. He looked out at Paul, who stared in amazement, then to the girls of Troop 149.

Jeremy knew he had to say something, but where should he start?

Before he could figure out that part of things, someone in the audience began to boo. A few others booed as well and that led to even more booing. Jeremy didn't try to stop them. He knew he deserved it. He closed his eyes and let everyone's anger wash over him. As he stood there, he felt someone move to his side. He looked to see Slater. Jeremy was glad to have him there, like his presence gave him the security of a forest rather than him being a single tree.

The insults kept on coming and the boys let the people have their fill. When the room began to quiet down, Jeremy steeled himself to say something but the microphone was gone. Margaret had it in her hands.

"Ladies and gentlemen," she said. "Before anyone decides what to do, I'd like to say a few words."

Jeremy leaned over. "Margaret, what are you doing?"

She covered the microphone. "Shut up before you screw things up even more."

That got a little laugh from the crowd.

Margaret started again. "Ladies and gentlemen, fellow Cadets, parents, and interested citizens. My name is Margaret Parsley and I have been a Cupcake Cadet since I was six years old. That makes this my sixth year and there is nothing I treasure more than my experiences with my troop.

"I'll admit I've known these two were not who they claimed to be for a few weeks now. The truth is I wanted to prove that girls are better than boys, that I could crush them." Her shoulders sagged, her head hung low. "And that goes against every value the Cupcake Cadets has tried to teach me."

The auditorium echoed with that last line while Margaret gathered her thoughts.

"And these *boys* . . . even though they violated Rule B1012-A Section Four of the Cupcake Cadet Code of Conduct . . . even though they nearly poisoned us with their terrible pie . . . even though they botched our field hockey game . . . and even though they practically drowned every single Cadet in Troop 149 . . ."

She looked at them.

"Not only did they help me design an awesome boat in thirty minutes, but they threw together a fund-raiser that propelled our troop to record sales." She shook her head. "I can't believe I'm going to say this, but I'm proud to call Jeremy and Slater my troop members. Even though they are not girls, I am proud to call them my sisters."

Jeremy's eyebrows furrowed. He had a strange feeling of not quite knowing how to feel, of all sorts of emotions rushing to the surface at once.

Just then, Mrs. Sanchez, too-red lipstick and all, tore the microphone from Margaret's hand. "That's all very nice and good," she said. "Now, all of you can get off the stage. You are disgraces to your uniforms."

Margaret glanced at Jeremy and considered for a moment. Then, she stared right at Mrs. Sanchez. She removed her tam and her sash and placed them on the podium.

And with that, Margaret walked out of the auditorium.

Jeremy looked to Ms. Rendell, who he expected would put an end to this nonsense. But she only shook her head sadly. "Why don't you just go on home?" she said. "We can talk about this tomorrow."

Jeremy made his way between the kiddie pools, through a sea of angry stares, to the lobby. On his way to the door, he heard a voice.

"Hey, Bender."

It was Paul Vogler.

Jeremy stopped. Even the most vicious of wedgies— hanging from the school flagpole with sandy underwear in a snowstorm—wouldn't compare with the pain he was feeling now. "What, Paul?"

"You called your stupid boat the *MEGAWEDGIE*?"

Jeremy only shrugged, resigned to what was coming next.

Then a grin spread across Paul's face. "You weirdos made my day. That was just too dang funny."

Jeremy shook his head and chased after Margaret.

From Little Boats to Big Boats

No one ever did figure out who destroyed Margaret's windjammer. Most people believed it was one of the brutes from Troop 224, a few others thought it might have been an inside job, that one of the girls from Troop 149 actually did the deed. In the darkest hours of the night, girls were known to whisper that it might have been Mrs. Sanchez who did it. Of course, in the end it didn't really matter. Margaret's boat was destroyed, along with her four-year winning streak.

But after that, things changed.

"Toss the wrench, will you?" Margaret said, wiping the grease from her hands with a rag. "I've got to tighten this belt."

Jeremy carefully handed Margaret the socket set. He didn't want to risk scratching the mahogany of his father's Chris-Craft. They had been working on it for three weeks now and were making real progress on the engine rebuild.

As they had made their way home after being ejected from the Windjammer Whirl, Margaret and Jeremy got to talking. After Jeremy thanked Margaret for standing up for him and Slater, they took turns sharing what they would have done with the prize money. Margaret had planned to put it toward a new computer and a design program so she could build an even better windjammer next year. Then Jeremy told Margaret all the gritty details about his father's boat—the damage he and Slater had caused and what it would take to fix it. When he mentioned it was an antique Chris-Craft, Margaret's mood lifted.

"I love Chris-Crafts!" she cried out. "They're my favorite boats!"

They had been working together ever since.

After admitting her knowledge of Jeremy and Slater's plot to the Cupcake Cadet High Council in Missoula, Montana, Margaret had been allowed to return, but only after writing a two-thousand-word essay on ethics. That was fine by her. Margaret had earned a Wicked Wordsmith Caliber Badge for the essay anyway, and it had been published in the local paper. Of course, the boys didn't continue their Cupcake Cadet careers. They had to turn in their badges immediately.

Paul was back to his old antics, giving noogies and book slaps in the hallways of the Thomas Scolari Academy for Boys, but Jeremy liked to think the noogies were a little less knuckly and the book slaps a little less slappy. Paul also refused to call them by their names any longer, preferring to stick with Jenna and Samantha.

Slater decided that building (or in this case, rebuilding) boats wasn't for him and bowed out of the project, opting instead for practicing his skateboard tricks and learning new dance moves in order to stay one step ahead of Angelina. He graced them with his presence quite often, though, typically propping his feet on a desk.

"Has anyone seen the sealant for the bilge pump bolts?" Angelina poked her head up from the engine compartment.

Slater hopped up. "I'll find it!"

"Hey," Angelina said, pointing to his face as he handed her the sealant. "Your lip gloss is wearing off. Want to try my Sour Apple Surprise?"

"Oh, stuff it," Slater said.

With no prize money to speak of, Jeremy finally had to admit to the damage he had done to the Chris-Craft. After looking it over and blowing his stack for a while, his father decided that an appropriate punishment would be for Jeremy to rebuild the engine. Jeremy would be responsible for the repairs, but he had to check in between each step for inspection of what he had already done and to describe in detail what he was going to do next. With Margaret and Angelina helping out, it was going a lot faster than expected. And the girls were earning Cupcake Cadet Mechanical Marvel Caliber Badges to boot.

The prize money from the Windjammer Whirl was another matter entirely. After arguing over the results and who should receive the award, the home office in Missoula, Montana, decided that no one would get it. Neither team acted in a way becoming of Cupcake Cadets, and even though there were quite a few innocent victims, cupcakes in the pan together bake together. Instead of one team walking away with the cash, the full amount would be donated to a local women's shelter. In the future, a trophy would be awarded and the prize money given to the charity of the winning team's choice.

Jeremy surveyed the icehouse, his eyes resting on the framed photo that hung over his desk. It was the picture of him and Slater dressed as Cupcake Cadets, the one Margaret had taken on their disaster of a camping trip. Margaret had presented it to Jeremy the first day she came over to work on the boat. She claimed she had deleted the file from her phone, but there was a distinctly Margaret-like twinkle in her eye when she said it.

Jeremy drew in a deep breath. The smell of motor oil filled his lungs. It was a smell he was growing to like. A lot.

"Hey," he called over to Margaret. "Do you have a three-quarter-inch socket? I'm trying to get this railing back on."

"You need thirteen-sixteenths, stupid." Margaret tossed it to him.

Really, she more like chucked it at his head. . . .

But at least it was chucked with a smile.

Acknowledgments

There is an old song I don't like by Bette Midler called "Wind Beneath My Wings." If you know anything about science, it's the wind *above* the wings that generates lift and allows for flight. So I'd like to take a moment to thank all the people who have been the wind above my wings. . . .

Thanks to my agent, Linda Pratt. Linda went that extra mile when she read my first manuscript nearly a decade ago. Know that not only did you steer me in the right direction, but you gave me the belief that I could actually do this.

Megathanks go my editor, Alessandra Balzer, and the great team at Balzer + Bray, including Donna Bray, Sara Sargent, and Emilie Polster. You guys have been awesome. I can't help but feel as though our journey is only beginning. Heck, I'd stay on board just for the awesome lunches (but don't tell Linda that).

Thanks to all the writer friends who served as my eagle eyes when mine were too bleary to edit any longer: Loree Griffin Burns, Nancy Castaldo, Julia DeVillers, Rose Kent, Liza Martz, Kate Messner, Coleen Paratore, and Leonora Scotti. A special thanks to all of my writer friends who have not yet been discovered. I know how bleak things can look some days. Keep plugging away and keep raising the bar for yourselves. You guys are my Northern Lights, always keeping me enthralled and inspired!

And of course, thanks to my family, who number too many to list here. But let me give a shout-out to all my nieces and nephews. Jenna and Samantha, I used your names in this book, but that's where the similarities between you two and Jeremy and Slater end. Lindsey, Evan, and Avery, don't fret. I'll save your names for some future book!

And to Elaine, Ethan, and Lily, who alone provide enough wind *above* my wings to keep me high in the stratosphere!